The Experiment

Even the book morphs!
Flip the pages
and check it out!

Look for other **ANIMORPHS**® titles by K.A. Applegate:

the andalite chronicles

The Hork-Bajir Chronicles

The Experiment

K.A. Applegate

AN
APPLE
PAPERBACK

SCHOLASTIC INC.
New York Toronto London Auckland Sydney
Mexico City New Delhi Hong Kong

The author wishes to thank Amy Garvey for her
help in preparing this manuscript.

For Michael and Jake

Cover illustration by David B. Mattingly

ISBN 0-590-76261-3

12 11 10 9 8 7 6 5 4 3 2 1   9/9 0 1 2 3 4/0

Printed in the U.S.A.   40

First Scholastic printing, April 1999

CHAPTER 1

My name is Aximili-Esgarrouth-Isthill.

It is not a human name. It is an Andalite name. Not that humans reading this are likely to know what an Andalite is. I am the only one here on Earth.

No, that is not completely true. There is one other. But he is not the Andalite he once was. He is now the host body to the Yeerk who holds the rank of Visser Three. Andalites call him the Abomination.

My duty is to someday destroy him.

I am only an *aristh*, a cadet. But as any Andalite who ever reads this will know, Andalite custom demands that I avenge my brother's death. Elfangor was a warrior and prince. Visser Three murdered him.

I suppose I thought that Elfangor would live forever. He was fearless. Honorable. Perfect. It was a lot for a brother to live up to because I am not any of those things.

But the memory of my brother is why I look forward to the day when I destroy Visser Three. It is not simply a matter of duty. I cared very deeply for my brother.

And I am not the only one who wants to destroy him and the other Yeerks who have invaded Earth. Before he died, Elfangor gave five human youths the power to morph. As well as the truth about why they need this power.

Now these five humans are the only ones resisting the Yeerk invasion. Fighting to stop the Yeerks from enslaving the entire human race. Fighting to stop them from crawling into human brains and taking over all thoughts, actions, and memories.

They are also the only ones who know about me.

They are my people now — the only people I have here, so far from home. I am grateful for their friendship. I respect them, too, which might be more important. But Tobias is the only one I might consider a true *shorm*.

A *shorm* is a deep friend, someone who knows everything there is to know about you. The word comes from the Andalite's tail blade, which looks something like what you may know as a scorpion's tail. A *shorm* is someone you would trust to put his tail blade against your throat.

Even though Tobias does not have a tail blade — or hooves, stem eyes, and fur, the way Andalites do — he is almost one of us. Elfangor was his father, and, as strange as it is to think of, I am, in Earth terms, Tobias's uncle.

But I think it is the fact that he is almost as unique on this planet as I am that makes us close. Choosing life as a red-tailed hawk has set Tobias apart from everything he once knew.

We are both unique on this planet, and both very much alone.

There are times at night, as I search the dark sky for the home star, when I think about my real people, my family. I think about a life that might have been very different from the one I am living now, here on a distant planet, far from everything I once knew.

The others, Prince Jake, Cassie, Rachel, and Marco, all have homes and families. Only Tobias and I do not. Tobias lives in a meadow that is his territory. And I, until recently, did not even have that limited amount to call my own.

But now I have made my life a bit more comfortable. I have constructed a sort of scoop — what we Andalites consider to be a home.

Like any scoop, it is mostly open, with only a small area covered by a semispherical roof. And in my case the scoop had to be very small so that I could fold the roof down and erase all visual evidence of it.

I had only a few things in the scoop. A *World Almanac* that my friends had given me. A photograph of a delicious cinnamon bun. Some human clothing. And one other thing only recently acquired. One very important other thing that has changed my life.

A television.

CHAPTER 2

Television. Or as most humans say, TV.

Ah, yes: TV!

I never expected it to be so compelling. At first I thought it would only be useful. I would watch the behavior of the humans on the flat, square screen and listen to them speak. When I am in human morph, I need to be able to seem entirely human.

But it is so much more than merely useful. It is a window into the human soul. Technologically it is laughable, of course, but when you take into account the stunning array of programs, it rivals the cinnamon bun itself as the finest creation of human society.

Tobias, too, enjoys TV. He comes every day to

5

watch a show with me. It is called *The Young and the Restless.* It is very educational, though I remain confused as to the cause of so much restlessness.

TV allows me to observe much more human behavior than I see at the mall. I am still wondering why humans put their mouths together. And why they seem to enjoy it. My first thought was that they were transferring food. But that seems not to be the case.

<Look, Tobias! Victor and Nikki are doing that thing again!> I pointed at the screen. <They do this very often.>

<Uh-huh.> His hawk eyes were trained on the little screen as Victor tightened his arms around Nikki. <It's called kissing, Ax-man. Just like yesterday. And the day before. Kissing. Everyone does it. Of course, you need lips.>

<I know what it is called. And the role of lips is self-evident. I simply do not know *why* it is performed.>

<Ah. Well . . .> Tobias rearranged his wings noisily. <It's definitely got a purpose. By the way, Marco's heading this way.>

<Yes, I know,> I said. <I saw him two minutes ago, although he is trying not to be seen.>

<I heard him *three* minutes ago and saw him *four* minutes ago,> Tobias said.

Tobias is competitive when it comes to his senses. His hearing and sight are both better than mine. But I am able to look in all directions simultaneously, something he cannot do.

<You did not,> I said.

<Did so,> Tobias countered.

"Nothing likes the joys of daytime TV, huh?" Marco said, stomping up through the underbrush.

<Did not,> I said to Tobias.

Marco grinned at me. "Snuck up on you, didn't I?"

<Yeah, right, Marco,> Tobias said tolerantly.

Marco laughed. He knew he had not surprised us. His claim to have snuck up on us was human humor. It is inexplicable, and Andalite readers should simply resign themselves to never understanding.

<And by the way, why are you not in school, young man?>

"Hey, I can't be controlled by 'the man's' arbitrary schedules. I come and go as I please. I am free. No one holds me down."

<Teacher conference?> Tobias said.

"Yeah, they let us out early. So. What's on the tube? Is this . . . Whoa! Who's *that*? And does she always walk around wearing a towel?"

<Well, I'm hungry. I gotta go find a mouse.

See you, Ax-man. Later, Marco,> Tobias said, and then he spread his wings and was gone.

"Watching a soap, huh?" Marco said, nodding his head.

<Soap?> I was confused. <No. This show is about humans who are both young and restless.>

Marco sighed. "Whatever you call it, it basically reeks, you know. I think it's time I introduced you to some better programming, Ax. *Buffy. Party of Five*, maybe. *Cops. South Park.* Something, anything better than this. Although *she* is hot."

<Yes, she is hot. This is why she often wears less artificial skin.>

"Yeah, well, I think you may have your cause and effect turned around there. Hey, you know what you need? A *TV Guide.*"

I bristled. <I understand how to operate the TV. Human technology is —>

"Take it easy!" Marco held up his hands. "Everything with you has got be literal. *TV Guide* is a little book that tells you what shows are on, and when. Come on, I'm bored. Let's cruise."

The notion of a guide to all that TV had to offer was attractive. But I would have to morph my human form to go into the town.

<Perhaps we could obtain cinnamon buns as well,> I suggested.

8

"Why not? Maybe we'll run into Jake at the mall. He can buy."

Every morph is a surprise. The last time I morphed to human, my own more or less humanoid parts, my head and arms, changed last. This time they were first.

I felt teeth growing beneath my lower face. In fact, my entire human mouth, consisting of a hinged jaw, teeth, tongue, and saliva-producing glands, was fully formed before lips appeared.

Lips form an open hole in the bottom third of a human face. The hole is used for eating and for forming mouth sounds. As well as kissing, spitting, vomiting, and belching.

Humans do a great deal with their mouths, most of it rather pointless.

My more numerous fingers disappeared, melting into ten stronger, thicker human fingers. My stalk eyes retracted into my head, leaving me unable to see behind me without either turning my head or turning my entire body.

My front legs shriveled away, leaving me to perch precariously on my two hind legs. Of course, humans have only two legs, and no tail at all. So they go through life constantly on the verge of falling over.

My blue fur was the last to go, replaced by my own particular shade of human skin. Human skin comes in a variety of shades, none of them attractive.

At least not to me. If you are a human, you must find something attractive about your fellow humans. Humans who are young and restless are almost continuously in a state of attraction to others.

When I was fully human — awkward, slow, and devoid of natural weapons — I put on my artificial skin. Humans call it clothing.

"I am ready," I said, making mouth sounds. "R-r-r-ready. Red. E. Red. E."

"How about putting on a shirt?" Marco asked.

"The men who are young and restless do not wear shirts. I am young. And I am occasionally restless."

"Ax?"

"Yes, Marco?"

"Put on a shirt."

I did. Then I folded my scoop down so that nothing, including the TV, would be visible. Not even to a human walking directly over the spot.

I walked with Marco out of the woods, across the farthest fields of Cassie's farm, and toward the mall. It took a long time. Humans walk very slowly, a result of having only two legs and no tail.

We crossed fields and then walked along a street — a path for cars. Then . . .

"Well, hello, Marco. Hey, Ax," someone called.

Marco stopped short and looked around, turning his entire human head in order to see in different directions. "Who said that?"

"Here, Marco."

I turned my human head to follow the voice. It was a truck painted with the word "FedEx." And it was talking to us.

CHAPTER 3

"What is this, *Candid Camera*?" Marco said.

"No. I believe it is a hologram," I said. It was the logical explanation. Trucks — which are large-wheeled vehicles used by humans to transport what they call "stuff" — do not have the power of speech.

And in any case, I recognized the particular qualities of that voice.

Marco made a disgusted face. "Hologram? Is that you, Erek?"

"Who else? Come on in. You're not being watched."

"There's a woman right across the street looking at us!"

"She's one of us, Marco," Erek said.

Marco and I walked directly into the side of the truck. I stepped through the blue and red letters to see Erek King.

He was not in his usual guise as a human boy, since he was using his holographic emitter to create the truck. Instead he appeared as the Chee android he really is.

The Chee are a race of highly sophisticated androids created by a race called the Pemalites. The creators are gone. Only their creations remain, posing as humans.

The Chee are programmed with specific traits. Nonviolence is one of those traits. And as much as Erek despises the Yeerks, and as powerful as he is, he must limit his anti-Yeerk activities to espionage.

He and his fellow Chee are quite effective in that area.

"A Federal Express truck?" Marco said. "Isn't that copyright infringement?"

Erek formed a metallic grin. "They can call my lawyer: He was Moses' law professor."

The Chee are also very, very long-lived.

"I have news," Erek said, serious now.

"Well, I didn't think you set this up to invite us over for pizza," Marco muttered.

"Let him speak, Marco," I said gravely, touching his arm. Jack, who is one of the youngest and most restless, does this often, when he is trying to be understanding. Marco and Erek stared at me.

"The Yeerks," Erek said finally. "We've learned they've used several fronts to purchase an animal testing laboratory and a meatpacking plant."

"Huh?"

"A meatpacking plant?" I repeated. "Meeeeet? Meeeetpacking?"

"It's where humans take animals — cows, pigs, chickens — to be slaughtered and then packaged for sale in the supermarket," Erek explained.

"Are you telling me I should worry about where my next Big Mac is coming from?" Marco said.

"We're not sure. We don't really know what they're doing with either facility. But we do know that they were purchased at about the same time, so we're certain there must be a connection."

"When did they acquire these facilities?" I asked him. "Fa-sill-it-tees." It was a good word for mouth-sounds. So many syllables.

"About a year ago." Erek shook his android head. "Unfortunately, we just learned about the purchase. The Yeerks are being extremely secretive about these projects."

Marco sighed. "You know, Erek, bumping into you is never a picnic. Why do we care if the Yeerks want to make burgers for a living?"

"I don't know," Erek admitted. "Maybe you don't care. But the Yeerks wouldn't be this secretive if it were nothing to worry about."

"You said they also had a laboratory," I prompted. "What is its purpose?"

"Don't know that, either."

"Let me ask you this: How about if we just forget all about this and don't tell Jake, and we all go to the mall and see how many cinnamon buns Ax can eat before he explodes?"

"I have already performed that experiment," I said.

Marco nodded. "Okay, then I guess we go tell Jake and the others and launch off into some dumb mission that'll end up with me screaming and running for my life. Sound good?"

"You could always go catch a burger instead," Erek said brightly.

Marco shook his head bitterly. "They're messing with the burgers, man. Now it's definite: The Yeerks must be destroyed."

CHAPTER 4

I had planned on an afternoon and evening of watching TV. But Rachel assured me that on Tuesday there was never anything on.

"Nothing but lame sitcom reruns this week," she said. "You're not missing anything."

<There are always *These Messages*,> I pointed out.

"These what?"

<The shorter shows that are displayed between longer shows. *These Messages*. They are often my favorites. "Zestfully clean! Zestfully clean! You're not fully clean unless you're Zestfully clean!" So much information condensed into so brief a format. So much emotional intensity.>

"You're starting to scare me, Ax."

In any case, Prince Jake had decided that we should act immediately to discover what, if anything, the Yeerks were doing at the animal testing laboratory and meatpacking plant.

We had all assembled at Cassie's barn to prepare for the mission.

Cassie's barn is called the Wildlife Rehabilitation Clinic. She and her father offer medical treatment to injured nonhuman animals. Nonhuman animals filled cages all around us. Many of them were creatures I had morphed.

When I say we "all" assembled, I mean, of course, Prince Jake, our leader, a male who is distinguished by being taller than the others; Rachel, a female who is considered beautiful by humans and held in awe by her fellow Animorphs for her bravery; Cassie, the most knowledgeable and gentlest of the group; and Tobias, Marco, and me.

Six of us. All with morphing power but very little else to oppose the Yeerk invasion of Earth.

It is an impossible situation, of course. But it has been impossible from the start. And we are not dead yet. If I were dead, I could hardly be expected to be communicating.

That was humor.

I believe.

<Meat? What do they want with meat?> Tobias demanded from his perch in the rafters.

"What, you're asking me?" Marco said. "Like I know? Erek just said they have this lab where they do animal testing and this meatpacking plant. That's all I know."

"Well this is just stupid," Rachel commented. "Meat? Animal testing? Why?"

"They're cleverly infiltrating Mickey D's to learn the secret of 'special sauce,'" Marco said.

"Mayonnaise, catsup, and relish," Rachel grumbled. "Big secret."

"Poison the food supply?" Cassie suggested as she forced a medicine down the throat of a goose. "Kill a lot of people?"

<No,> I said. <If the Yeerks wished to kill a lot of humans they could simply use their Dracon beams from orbit to ignite the atmosphere and incinerate all life on the planet.>

Everybody turned to stare at me.

"Well. There's a happy thought," Marco said with what I believe is a tone of voice called "sarcasm."

"We won't get any answers sitting around here guessing," Prince Jake said. He sighed. "Rachel? I am messed up in old lady Chambers's class. Did you take decent notes?"

"Yeah. I can E-mail them over to you after we get back. But it's like a whole bunch of stuff."

Prince Jake sighed again and rubbed his eyes. "Okay look, let's go get this over with fast or

I'll end up spending the weekend doing a makeup paper, which would seriously stink."

"What exactly are we doing?" Cassie asked.

"We're just going to take a look at this animal testing lab. See what's what."

<What is animal testing?> I asked.

"They get a bunch of animals together and give them quizzes from magazines," Marco said. "You know, like 'How Shy Are You?' and 'Is He Mr. Right?'"

I hesitated before responding. It was probably humor.

<I suspect you are making a joke. But I am not certain.>

"No one ever is," Rachel said with a laugh.

"Animal testing labs are facilities where humans use species similar to our own to test the effects of drugs or whatever," Cassie said. "They have to see if something is safe for humans, so they see first if it's safe for animals."

<That sounds prudent —> I began to say. But Cassie was not finished.

"They are also about as close to hell as anything humans create," Cassie said.

"Uh-oh. Here we go." Marco groaned. "Quick! Everyone find a tree to hug."

"Look, I'm not a fanatic on this," Cassie said. "I'm not against testing some new AIDS drug or a cancer cure. But there are labs where makeup is

19

tested, only they test it in ways that cause the test animals to go blind. And even when they test for serious stuff, they should try to make the animals' lives a little less horrible."

"Yeah, get them TV," Marco said. "No, wait, that might be cruel."

Cassie's eyes flashed and she bit her lower lip. Cassie is seldom angry. But I believe this was a display of anger.

Rachel saw the same thing. "Marco? Try: Shut up. Cassie? I love you, but this isn't about saving the lab rats. We have a mission here. So let's just go and get it over with."

"Rachel's right, we can debate animal testing some other day," Prince Jake said. "Let's just do this. In, out, and right back."

<After *These Messages.*>

CHAPTER 5

We morphed to birds of prey. My own is called a northern harrier. Birds of prey are especially useful for observation because they have incredibly acute vision as well as excellent hearing.

Once morphed, we flew toward the animal testing laboratory.

The sun was going down, causing the wild effusion of colors, primarily red and gold that sometimes occurs at sunset or sunrise.

I was afraid of what I might find at the animal testing laboratory. Sometimes, when exposed to what humans consider science, I inadvertently offend my friends. I am often tempted to explain human errors.

We flew over a large street called Broad, above a park called Willow, and beyond, toward an area where many buildings had transparent windows replaced by opaque sheets of wood.

Few humans were visible. But we saw a great deal of garbage. Garbage is an important human product.

Marco kept grumbling about the online chat with the cast of *The X-Files* he was missing. "Online" is a primitive human method of communicating in short, truncated, interrupted sentences with anonymous individuals.

Humans have several means of communicating in uninterrupted form with known persons, but many prefer "online."

Like much of human technology, it is inexplicable.

<Yeah, well, I'm missing precious time trying to figure out how quadratic equations work,> Cassie answered.

<Is that it? Is that the place?> Rachel asked. She was above me, to my left.

<That's the right corner,> Tobias said. <Must be.>

<Doesn't look too sinister. Yeah, I can see a sign. That's it,> Prince Jake said. <Your basic office park.>

We flew to the edge of the large empty area where humans place their cars. The cars were gone. It was the time of day when humans leave their work and go home to consume food.

Several groups of young trees had been planted around the empty lot, so we perched among their branches.

Most of the buildings seemed empty. But one, set apart from the others, was surrounded by a ten-foot-high fence made of ingenious inter-looped metallic strands and topped with spirals of sharp-spiked wire.

Across a small parking area sat a plain, two-story brick building, deep in shadows cast by the low slanting rays of the sun. Behind it, parallel to Broad Street, was undeveloped land thick with mature trees.

The windows of the building were all closed and protected by vertical bars. The doors were heavy steel. An armed guard sat in a structure that looked like a miniature human house, just behind a gate that was set into the fence.

<Security,> Rachel said with a derisive laugh.

<Some small morph would be the way to go,> Prince Jake said. <But what? Even a fly can't get through a locked metal door.>

<And you know the Yeerks inside are going to be suspicious of any kind of animal,> Cassie added. <Even the ones they're testing.>

<And we do not know . . .> I paused for a long moment, the way I had seen Victor Newman

23

do. Whenever he does this, the TV camera zooms in on his face. <. . . what *kind* of animals are being tested in there.>

Five bird-of-prey heads turned to look at me. They stared at me the way Marco and Erek had earlier.

<Ax? You okay?>

<Yes, but I must maintain silence till we go to *These Messages*.>

<He's been watching soaps,> Marco explained.

<Ohhhh. He's doing a soap-take!> Rachel said.

<A what?>

<A soap-take. At least that's what I call it. At the end of a scene. You know how the actors all just freeze and stare and wait for . . . well, for "these messages"?>

<Those are my favorites,> I said. *<These Messages.>*

ZAAP!

We all jerked in surprise.

Tobias said, <A rabbit.>

The animal was dead. I could see that its breathing had stopped.

<Electric fence,> Cassie said.

<Electric?> I laughed. <I doubt it very much. If this facility is run by the Yeerks, then it is certainly a shock-front force field. The fence is

24

merely incidental, a deception. The force field will extend in an unbroken dome over the entire facility. A large energy expenditure.>

<He's right,> Tobias said. <Look around. Dead sparrow over there. A rat. Too much road-kill.>

<Great,> Rachel muttered.

<That means the only way to get onto the grounds is past the security guard, right in the front door. And I don't know how we're going to do that.>

<Look!> Cassie said. A large white truck, probably thirty human feet long, passed the trees where we were hidden and pulled up to the gate.

I could not see the contents of the truck, although I was sure it contained some sort of "stuff."

<I'll listen in.> Tobias opened his wings and flew to a solitary tree just outside the fence.

The truck driver rolled down his window and presented the guard with a rectangular board with paper affixed. The guard scrutinized it for a moment before pushing a button in the little building where he sat. The gate opened with a rusty whine.

The truck started down the drive and disappeared behind the building.

<Let's follow the fence around and see what he's unloading,> Rachel suggested.

<Wait.> Tobias returned, landing on a nearby branch, and regarded us with his intense hawk's eyes. <The truck's loaded with chimpanzees. There's no window between the cab and the back so I couldn't actually see them, but I heard the driver say he had the six chimps they called for.>

<Chimps?> Prince Jake frowned. <Why chimpanzees?>

<Chimpanzees would maybe be used for some kind of behavioral research,> Cassie said. <If it was medical they'd probably use rats or rhesus monkeys.>

<Perhaps the chimps will be transferred to the meatpacking plant?> I asked innocently.

<Oh, gee, let's hope not,> Prince Jake said.

<You never know,> Cassie said darkly.

<Yeah, where do you think they get jerky from?> Marco asked.

<The driver said something about being back around four tomorrow,> Tobias added.

<Six more chimps?> Rachel wondered.

<On their way to nothing good,> Cassie said thoughtfully. <But that's our way in. We go as the chimps.>

<Can we acquire chimpanzees at The Gardens?> Prince Jake wondered.

<All we know is that they have "chimps" in that truck. But that may not mean specifically chimpanzees. I mean, the driver may not exactly

be a primatologist. Could be rhesus monkeys, could be howler monkeys, could be bonobo chimps or some other subspecies, so —>

<Wait. Here comes the truck.> Rachel trained her eagle eyes on it. <Hey! It has a parking sticker from the university. Maybe that's where it starts out.>

<Okay, so they come down the highway, get off across from the new mega-mall, come up Broad Street, right?> Prince Jake said. He was silent for a while, deep in thought. Then, <I think I've got an idea. Could work.>

<Is it an insanely dangerous, nearly suicidal idea?!> Marco asked brightly.

<Yep. Sure is.>

CHAPTER 6

The others had spent the day in their human school. Tobias and I had spent the day watching TV, and then watching cars go along a road and into and out of a tunnel.

A tunnel is an underground road. Humans build them to pass beneath rivers, or to pass beneath roads or buildings whose presence evidently surprises them.

Planning ahead is not a great human virtue.

The road was lined with restaurants named Wendy's, Taco Bell, and Fuddruckers. There were also areas where automobiles were displayed for sale. And there was the store where one would not pay a lot for that muffler.

Prince Jake and the others arrived to meet us already in seagull morph, wheeling down from above. They were almost invisible against the clouds. White on white.

I had been in that same morph all afternoon, except for necessary demorphing. Tobias was in his own red-tailed hawk body, resting atop a nearby denuded tree hung with wires. Tobias could not manage to stand directly on the wires.

It had been a long day. Prince Jake had impressed on us the need for precise planning. And it had been necessary for me to demorph and remorph several times. In a Dumpster, which is a large box filled with stuff humans no longer want.

<We all set?> Prince Jake asked as he swooped down to join me.

<Yeah,> Tobias said. <If you need to demorph there's a delightful Dumpster that Ax has been enjoying.>

<No, we're good. Although . . . Whoa! Doritos!>

<Forget it. Empty bag. Ax already ate them. I'm going topside so I can give you all a heads-up.>

Tobias opened his wings and flapped away above the road, above the bright signs of restaurants that served delicious grease and salt.

Seagull morph is very useful since it is ubiquitous. Like the birds called pigeons, seagulls may go almost anywhere unremarked.

But there is a downside: The seagull has a relentless, obsessive interest in any food that has been thrown away. It is almost as distracting as being human.

<Everyone clear on the plan?> Prince Jake asked.

<Yeah. We pretty much hurtle to our deaths, right?> Marco said.

<Oh, quit your whining, you big baby,> Rachel said.

We waited near the Dumpster till we heard faint thought-speak coming from high above. <The truck is en route. Passing Church Street.>

<What was the time on the tunnel, Ax?> Prince Jake asked.

<Between four and seven of your minutes, Prince Jake,> I said. <We timed it repeatedly. With this degree of traffic we estimate transit time through the tunnel will be closer to seven minutes.>

<Ax? Don't call me Prince. Everyone set?>

<Here it comes!> Cassie said.

The truck appeared, coming down the street toward us.

<We catch him at the light,> Prince Jake reminded us. <Everyone careful, okay? This

could go bad on us pretty easily. So pay attention.>

<Especially if he doesn't get stopped for that light,> Cassie said. <Come on, light, change! Change!>

<It will change from green to yellow in exactly four seconds, Cassie, and I am of the opinion that the light mechanism does not respond to thought-speak pleas.>

The traffic slowed as the light in the intersection changed to yellow.

Yellow is the color of warning. I do not know why.

The delivery truck we had seen the night before was behind a smaller green truck. I heard noises indicating that the truck driver had engaged the pitifully primitive braking system.

<Now!> Prince Jake said.

One by one we flapped and caught the air current.

My legs tucked beneath me, I opened my wings wider and began to rise as a gusty breeze hit me. Even in the midst of a dangerous mission, I am aware of the fact that when I fly I feel even more free than I do when running across an open meadow.

<Down, Ax! Now!> I heard Rachel say.

Angling sideways to tack against the breeze, I watched as first Prince Jake and then Cassie swept their wings forward to slow down. Marco, Rachel, and I were right behind them, killing airspeed as we headed for the rumbling truck. Tobias was plummeting from high above, ready to follow.

The roof was smooth. I slid into Rachel as the indicator light changed and the truck began to pick up speed.

I felt the uneven vibrations of the engine as the truck proceeded through the intersection. I felt the pressure of the wind as the truck accelerated.

Suddenly what had seemed fairly simple began to seem troublesome.

<Okay, the tunnel's only two blocks away,> Prince Jake said, crouching to maintain his balance. <Start demorphing.>

<This is crazy!> Rachel shouted happily, squinting her beady seagull eyes as the truck's grime swirled around us.

<I am slipping,> I said.

<You and me both. More fun every minute,> Marco complained.

My bird legs were essentially useless at holding on in the face of a powerful wind. I collapsed my legs, opened my wings, and shaped them so as to create a downdraft. The downdraft held me down. But still I was sliding toward the back of the truck.

I needed to morph. Cassie had already started, and the additional weight helped to stabilize her position.

I focused on the demorph. My feathers melted into a gelatinous coating that began to sprout my natural fur. My stalk eyes sprouted from the top of the gull's small head. My beak shrank and withered to nothingness. The sliding stopped.

I looked back over the very close edge of the truck. A small car was nearby. The driver had apparently noticed the shifting mess of feathers, fur, and skin. His mouth hung open as he leaned forward to watch.

And just then, my tail sprouted to its full length.

WHAM!

The small car sideswiped a limbless tree used to elevate wires.

Screeeee! Cuh-RUNCH!

The small car came to a halt very suddenly, having run directly into a stopped car.

I turned my emerging stalk eyes forward again. I could see the dark arch of the tunnel just ahead. Cassie was fully human already. The others were mostly human, with a dusting of white feathers here and there. Tobias was also mostly human, although for him it was no longer his normal form.

Suddenly, we were in the tunnel. Darkness closed around me. The yellow tile ceiling was only inches above me!

I had not realized it would be so close. No room! If I raised an arm, it would be scraped along that soot-blackened ceiling.

And if I raised my head?

Woosh!Woosh!Woosh!Wooosh!

The ceiling made a sound as we passed beneath it.

I fought down the claustrophobia that is a part of any Andalite's heritage. *There is sufficient room,* I told myself. *There is sufficient air.*

And yet I did not feel that there truly was enough air or enough space. I could feel the pressure of tons of earth weighing me down. We were underground. Soon we would be underwater!

I lay there, my legs curled up beneath me, tail extended flat, upper body pressed low, and stared at the tiles flashing by above me.

And the noise! My head was reeling from the cacophony of magnified, echoed noises of engines and brakes and radios and horns.

I lay still and concentrated on breathing. There was plenty of air. Plenty of room. Plenty.

But I could not just lie there. We had to enter the truck. I would have to move.

"Okay, human chain time!" Cassie yelled to be heard above the constant shriek of noise.

It was the only way we had thought of to get into the back of the truck: by grasping hand to hand, hand to ankle. It is something humans, with their much stronger arms and more linear bodies, can do.

"Hold my feet and lower me over the back so I can open the door," Cassie yelled.

"I will go first," Prince Jake said.

"Not happening, Jake. You weigh twice what I do," Cassie said. "Don't distract me when I'm trying to be brave."

Cassie shimmied to the back edge of the roof as Prince Jake and Tobias clutched her ankles. Marco threw his arms around Prince Jake's waist, Rachel around Marco's. Lying beside this human chain, I braced with all four hooves against the slick roof and grabbed Prince Jake's ankles.

We had no real way to brace ourselves. We could only hope that our bodies, pressed flat, would create sufficient friction to resist the hurricane of wind.

"Lower!" Cassie shouted. "I can't quite reach!"

Carefully, the human-Andalite chain of bodies inched forward until the only visible part of Cassie was her bare feet.

35

"I'm there!" she cried. Then, "No lock!"

"No luck?"

"No *lock*!" she yelled, and there came a rolling sound as the door slid up into the roof.

We hauled Cassie back up. Cassie flipped positions. Still on her stomach, she swung her legs over the back of the truck and held on to the roof's edge as we clutched her wrists.

"Oh, man!" Cassie moaned.

"What?" Prince Jake demanded.

"Just 'Oh, man!'" Cassie said.

From inside the truck came a loud cry. "EYAH! EYAH! EYAH! Hoo hoo hoo!"

I was unclear as to the meaning, but I suspected they were noises emitted by the chimpanzees. Perhaps they were alarmed. I certainly was.

Cassie swung back and forth. And now another car was closing the distance behind us. It was dark in the tunnel, but still sufficiently light for the human in the car to clearly see that we were breaking into the truck.

The car was also close enough that if Cassie slipped, it would slam into her and most likely kill her instantly.

"Okay, let go of me!" Cassie yelled.

We released our grip.

"Aaaahhh!"

Thump!

"Owww! I'm okay. But owww!"

Cassie was inside the truck. Marco followed quickly. It was easier with someone inside to assist.

The driver behind us did not notice me, but he definitely noticed the others as they swung down into the truck. The driver was smiling, making a sort of pumping motion with his fist and yelling.

I believe what he yelled was, "Waaahhhh-hooh! Hoo! Hoo! Hoo!"

I am unclear as to the meaning. But I believe they were noises of approval. He cannot possibly have known our mission, of course, so I took it as a general approval of the notion of breaking into trucks. Or perhaps he merely enjoyed acrobatics.

The driver passed us by. And now it was my turn. Just one problem: I could not possibly support my own weight with my own arms and fingers.

I had to morph to human. And looking ahead, I could already see the far end of the tunnel.

We had used more time than we should have. I had only two minutes left.

CHAPTER 7

I morphed to human. I morphed very quickly.

In human morph I had only two eyes. This made it easier to ignore the tile still flashing by at shocking speed.

As soon as I had strong human arms I shoved my lower body over the edge of the truck. But something was wrong!

Too heavy! I could not hold on!

Numerous hands grabbed at me, slipped, tugged, grabbed again.

"Ax! You're still not morphed!"

My lower half was still mostly Andalite. Too large! Too heavy!

I felt my hands weakening. My fingers were

being pried open by the weight. I would fall onto the road. Humans would drive their cars over me. Possibly their trucks filled with "stuff" as well.

I was no longer concerned with the tile overhead. I was much more interested in the pavement below.

"Grab his tail!"

"I have a leg! He's morphing his leg! Ax, I . . ."

"EYAH! EYAH! EYAH! Ooog! Ooog!"

"Get him, get him, he's slipping!"

"He keeps morphing!"

"Hoo hoo hoo hoo hah ah HAH HAH HAH HAH!"

"Please make every effort not to drop me!" I cried.

"Okay, I got a human leg here," Rachel said.

Moments later, I was hauled inside the truck. Suddenly I felt no wind.

The truck emerged from the tunnel. I began to laugh.

"Are you okay, Ax-man?" Tobias asked.

"I am very well! Very, very well. Well-luh." There was nothing funny about eluding death, but there was certainly joy. And relief.

"'Please make every effort not to drop me.'" Marco repeated my plea, and now everyone laughed.

Rachel drew the door down. There was not

39

much light, but there was enough. And the relative quiet was very enjoyable.

I looked around at the inside of the truck. On either side of the truck, eight-foot-wide, four-foot-tall cages held shaggy, brownish-black creatures with hairless, surprisingly human, faces. Two were hunched forward, clutching the bars and screeching. The others had flattened themselves against the far walls, grimacing and pounding the floor.

"No bananas." Marco spread his hands wide in apology. One of the chimpanzees spit at him.

"We need to acquire them right away. Grab his foot, if you can," Prince Jake suggested.

"*You* grab his foot," Marco said. "I've been a gorilla. I know what our grandparents here can do when they get cranky."

"Here." Cassie had opened a sturdy plastic bin on the floor. "This'll help."

I began to demorph to Andalite form as Cassie cautiously held out a handful of grayish-brown pellets to one of the chimpanzees. The chimpanzee paused and seemed to sneer at her. The truck hit a bump. Cassie lurched forward and the chimpanzee drew back.

"It's okay," she murmured. "These are for you."

The chimpanzee regarded her solemnly. It

seemed to be deciding whether or not the food was a trick.

One giant finger extended through the bars of its cage, pointing at Cassie's palm. The creature's skin looked like tan leather. I heard Rachel inhale abruptly. Marco shimmied backward an inch. Beside him Tobias was demorphing to hawk form, watching the chimp intently.

"It's okay," Cassie repeated. "She's not going to hurt me. Here, girl." She reached forward slowly.

"Rachel? Get ready, in case we need firepower," Prince Jake warned.

"Not necessary," Cassie said. "This girl's just a sweetie. She'll be fine. Won't you, girl? No need to be upset. No."

The chimp paused again, considered, pursed its lips, and grunted. Without warning, it grabbed Cassie's wrist.

But Cassie is not easily bothered by non-human animals. Her other hand shot out and grabbed the chimp's enormous hand. Cassie focused, and the acquiring trance calmed the animal.

But Cassie herself was not entirely calm. She looked troubled. I could not tell why. I only noticed that for several seconds she seemed almost to be carrying on a silent argument with herself.

But then she focused again and the chimpanzee's eyelids drooped imperceptibly. Its muscles slackened. The food in its hand dropped to the floor as it slumped into the cage's bars.

The rest of us made contact while we could. We acquired the chimpanzee. Chimpanzees are a species closely related to humans but slightly more attractive, and with a superior method of locomotion that allows them to operate as two-footed or four-footed creatures.

"Okay, ticktock. We must be almost there. Keys?" Rachel asked.

"Here they are," Marco said, snatching a ring from a wall clip. "Let's hope these chimps don't attack as a good-bye gesture." He smiled at one of the soon-to-be-freed chimpanzees. "Loved you in all those old Tarzan movies."

"This stinks," Cassie said. "We shouldn't be turning them loose in a strange environment. We shouldn't be . . . never mind."

"Ah, I was wondering how long it would take," Marco said with a derisive grin.

<Look, a day running around the streets has got to be better than whatever the Yeerks have in mind for them,> Tobias said.

Prince Jake leaned toward the first cage, ready to open the door. "Here we go," he breathed, sliding the key into the padlock. "Freedom. At least till someone rounds you up."

I felt the truck grind to a stop.

"Now," Prince Jake said. "Ax? Stay out of sight. There may be cars right behind us."

Cassie and Marco slid the door up.

And the chimpanzee we had morphed, faced with freedom, decided to urinate.

CHAPTER 8

"Run away, already!" Marco yelled.

A truck was coming up behind us, slowing. Cars were alongside. Two children in one of the cars pointed at us and bounced up and down in their seats.

"Cassie, make them leave!" Marco pleaded.

Cassie scooped up a handful of food pellets and flung them toward the truck behind us. The chimpanzees merely stared. The driver of the truck leaned out of his window and said words I have been told are impolite.

<I've got this,> Tobias said. He flapped his wings furiously and launched himself toward the lead chimpanzee.

"Tseeer!" he screeched.

The lead chimp bounded away. The others tumbled after him. And now the truck driver behind us began to say words that were worse than impolite.

<Thought that might do it,> Tobias said smugly.

With a jerk that almost knocked me off my hooves, we were moving again.

Prince Jake yanked the door down, but before he did I saw one of the chimps climbing in the window of the truck while the driver exited quickly from the opposite door. A second chimp was bouncing maniacally on the roof of the car with the children. The children were screaming with joy. Their mother was also screaming, but perhaps not with joy.

"Okay, into the cages and morph," Prince Jake said. "Ax? How's our time?"

<I estimate we will arrive at the laboratory in three of your minutes.>

"Ax, don't make me tell you again: They're not *our* minutes," Marco said. "They are *everyone's* minutes. Just plain old minutes and . . . oh guh-ross." Marco wrinkled his nose disgustedly as he climbed into the nearest cage. "Someone call the manager. This cage is filthy."

"You guys go ahead," Cassie said. "I'll hang back to lock the doors behind you."

It made sense. Cassie was the quickest

morpher. And someone would have to lock the cages from the outside.

I closed my main eyes, trying to focus despite the lurch of the truck and the realization that we were very short on time. I focused my thoughts on the image of the chimp. Then I felt it begin.

My front legs melted into my torso as my back legs swelled into the powerful limbs of the chimp. My hooves split open into five-toed feet. My Andalite arms grew bulky with muscles. My hands exploded into leathery flesh and thick fingers.

I felt two faint blips as my hearts stopped beating, absorbed into the pounding heart of the chimp. Inside me — bones crunched, blood pumped, as a mass of organs and systems transformed from Andalite to primate.

My stalk eyes had already retracted, disappearing into the top of the chimp's head. Beneath the flattened nose that was similar to my own the chimp's mouth emerged. It was large and mobile and full of teeth.

I turned my head to squint at the others in the murky light while wiry brown fur sprouted over most of my body.

"Urrgghh," I grunted through the chimp's mouth, grabbing the bars of the cage. I tried again to speak.

<Interesting,> I said. <Though these bodies

are nearly identical to humans, they are incapable of coherent speech.>

<Yeah, that's why you never see chimpanzees running for president. They're smart enough. They just can't give a decent speech.>

Marco, of course. Humor, almost certainly. Although it occurred to me that I should perhaps check and see whether chimpanzees were accorded full citizenship.

I blinked my primate eyes and flexed my thick, powerful fingers. I felt . . . human. Like I was a four-foot-tall, almost two-hundred-pound, heavily muscled human.

And the mind? It was not exactly human, but it was similar. The same threads of curiosity, understanding, and emotion woven into a complex map. It was nothing like the single-minded hunger instinct of the shark, or the blind rush of sensory input that characterized the bat, for example.

Sentient? Self-aware? Able to hold abstract thoughts in its head?

Impossible to be sure. In morphing we acquire instinct, but instinct is less important when intelligence is more developed.

This mind had very little in the way of instinct. And I sensed a great deal in the way of intelligence.

The chimpanzee would be able to understand

that when the cage was locked, it would not be able to escape. The chimpanzee would understand that scratching its head repeatedly would not open the door, but it would make it feel better.

The Andalite part of me suddenly felt a little ill. I knew that chimpanzees were very close to humans on Earth's evolutionary scale. I later learned that ninety-seven percent of chimpanzee DNA is identical to human DNA.

Too close to human? *Sentient* close?

We have a rule — we Animorphs, I should say — that we do not morph humans or other sentient beings without permission. Had we just violated that belief?

Cassie circled the cages quickly to lock the cage doors. Then she ducked into the cage closest to the hook where Marco had found the keys. She reached through the bars, locked her own door, and tossed the keys on the floor beneath the hook.

"Hopefully the driver will think they fell off when he hit a bump," she said.

Cassie morphed with shocking speed.

I decided to ask her about the chimpanzee. Cassie is often the person most willing to examine deeper philosophical issues.

<Cassie, I am concerned by this morph,> I

said. <Is it sentient? Was it improper to acquire it?>

She said nothing. As though she had not heard me. Then she turned her dark chimpanzee eyes toward me. <Could it have given permission, do you think? Is it capable?> she asked rhetorically.

<No. I doubt that it could have understood the question,> I answered. <But you have not answered my question, Cassie. Is this creature sentient?>

Cassie said nothing and Marco laughed a thought-speak laugh. <You don't get it, Ax. See, Cassie's on her own private mission here. She wants to save the chimps. So her usual moralizing doesn't apply.>

It was a harsh thing to say. But Cassie made no answer.

<A silence fills the room,> Marco said sardonically. <Animal lovers. Typical. They care more about animals than they do about humans. If we were doing this for some other reason, we'd have Cassie giving us a bunch of crap about not using sentient creatures. But she's thinking she can maybe save some chimpanzees, so hey, if it's for the sake of animals —>

<Let it go, Marco,> Prince Jake interrupted.

Cassie said nothing in self-defense.

I did not know what to think. I could only assume that humans do not believe chimpanzees are sentient. Clearly, if they did believe it, they would not be keeping them imprisoned and using them for experimentation.

Yes, that made logical sense, I reassured myself.

On the other hand, it is sometimes the case that humans do not make logical sense.

CHAPTER 9

The truck slowed and then came to a stop.

When the door rolled up on its rusty hinges, the still-bright afternoon light flooded the truck. I squinted and shrank against the far wall of my cage.

"Okay, you monkeys, get ready," a large human grunted as he pulled himself into the truck.

I looked past him. A second human slid a ramp into place, connecting the truck to a large, open doorway. The doorway was elevated several feet above the ground. In fact, it matched the height of the back of the truck. Proving that sometimes humans are capable of planning ahead.

Just inside the building stood three men in white, loose-fitting artificial skin. Clothing. At their feet was a flat metal cart on wheels.

Marco and I were in the cages closest to the door. One of us would be the first to go.

The men lifted my cage, straining as they pulled it onto the cart. Once on the cart, they pushed me along the ramp.

I shifted uneasily behind the bars. Was I acting the part appropriately? What would a chimpanzee do under these circumstances?

<Everyone be kind of cool,> Cassie instructed. <These chimps were probably raised in captivity. They'd be somewhat used to all this.>

The vibrations caused by the cart's wobbly wheels against the ramp rattled through my legs and up my spine.

Inside the building, the cart turned a corner, guided by three pairs of human hands, and slid through an open door.

HooHoo He-YAH! He-YAH! Heeeee!

This new room was filled with other chimpanzees. All around me chimpanzees chattered wildly, screeching and jumping in cages that were mounted on the walls with thick steel braces. Clearly, they were unnerved by our intrusion.

Wheels whined against the floor as the cart stopped outside an empty cage. Two horizontal rows of four cages each lined the wall, the same one in which the door was located. Once in the cage, I would have difficulty seeing who was entering the room.

A human with a gray beard and small blue eyes referred to a chart that he had unclipped from the side of the cage. "Hello, Pumpkin. There's a good girl. How about a treat?" He held out a cookie frosted with white icing.

I sniffed carefully. Sugar.

A delicious treat? No doubt. But was it also heart-healthy and low fat? In *These Messages*, everything is heart-healthy and low fat.

What would taste be like to a chimpanzee? I was certain that the chimpanzee brain wanted the cookie. Oh yes, it wanted the cookie.

I grabbed it.

The man smiled. He unlocked the cage door.

I tensed again as each of my powerfully developed muscles stiffened in readiness. I felt the chimp's mouth stretching into the strange grimace-smile that to a chimpanzee indicates fear and displays teeth.

Teeth that were midway through munching one of the most delicious cookies I had ever tasted. In any form.

The man reached forward with sudden speed. He snapped a collar around my neck and grabbed one of my enormous hands.

53

No doubt the chimpanzee would have been afraid. But it was enjoying the cookie. So was the Andalite.

"Okay, Pumpkin," the bearded man said. "Here we go." As he swung with the arm that held mine, I found myself responding without thought. My legs pushed against the floor. My free hand clutched at the top of the cage door and pushed, too, as I vaulted toward the cage opposite me.

Then I was in. Another lock clicked into place as I swallowed the last cookie crumb and sat down.

"Good girl, Pumpkin," the man said. He handed me another cookie while the other men pushed my former cage out of the way. "Okay, let's go for the others."

I took a look around as the three men left to unload my friends. I appeared to be in some kind of holding room. It was covered by small white squares of a hard, somewhat shiny substance. Tiles, I believe they are called. There was a drain in the center of the floor.

Eight-human-foot-square cages lined the two longest walls, and one, about eight feet deep by fifteen feet wide, was set into the shorter wall to my right. To my left, against the other short wall, was a metal table covered with bins containing papers. Next to the table was a frosted glass door.

The big cage was empty of animal life, but held a tire swing, dull red rubber toys, and a thick rope with several knots. Someone had scribbled in bright colors on the concrete block walls.

The noise was deafening. I crouched against the back wall of my cage and covered my ears, somewhat overwhelmed. At least twenty chimpanzees were screaming and hooting, stamping their feet against the floors of their cages. I looked up as one directly opposite me took a mouthful of water from a squeeze bottle and sprayed it in my general direction.

Did they sense that I was different? That I was not quite all chimpanzee? Without really thinking about it, I jeered back in full chimpanzee screech. And then turned as the door opened again.

<I'm innocent, I tell you!> Marco cried in private thought-speak as he was wheeled into the room. <I can't do hard time! I'm innocent! You got the wrong guy! You can't keep me locked up! I want to call my lawyer!>

CHAPTER 10

< The big question is still: What are we doing here?> Cassie said, when at last all of us had been brought together.

<That's what we'll find out. Soon as these handlers leave,> Prince Jake said.

<Ticktock,> Rachel muttered. <We've been in morph for a long time now.>

"Clear chimp menagerie area," a voice said.

<Loudspeaker,> Cassie remarked. <Look at the handlers!>

The handlers were heading for the exit. They were moving quickly. Very quickly. In a hurry to be out of the room. I assumed they had somewhere else to be. The others made the same assumption.

We were all mistaken.

<Cassie. You want to demorph and bust us outta here?> Prince Jake asked. <The rest of us might as well stay in these morphs for now. Someone could come back in.>

<No problem,> Cassie said. <Then maybe Ax and Marco can get us into that computer over there. Maybe we'll learn what this is all about.>

I had not noticed a computer. It was outside of my limited range of vision. Cassie began swiftly demorphing.

I spent the time considering what we might find in the computer. I was confident that I could easily break any Yeerk security measures. But once into the system, I still might find nothing.

I watched Cassie's softer human features begin to emerge from the chimpanzee. Watched the fur melt and smooth out to form her own human skin. Watched her legs strengthen, her arms weaken.

Chimpanzees are proof of the unpredictability of evolution. Many humans think evolution involves improvement. Of course, it does not. It merely involves survivability. Often individual capabilities are lessened in the process of moving toward a survivable species. Humans are clearly weaker than chimpanzees. But their brains are much more capable.

Well, somewhat more capable.

Cassie was entirely human when the door opened. From the first tiny noise of the handle being moved, I realized our mistake. It wasn't that the handlers had somewhere else to be.

It was that the handlers didn't want to be here.

And when the door opened, I saw the reason why.

If there had been any slight doubt that the laboratory was Yeerk-run, the creature who stepped through the door followed by three cringing, terrified human-Controllers put an end to it.

He stepped boldly into the room. Swaggering like the conqueror he was.

He was Andalite in form. His host body is an old Andalite warrior named Alloran-Semitur-Corrass.

But he was no longer Alloran. He was no longer an Andalite at all, except in outer form.

He was Visser Three. The Abomination. The only Andalite-Controller in the galaxy.

I leaped at the bars, unable to control the urge. Visser Three did not flinch.

<Cassie!> Rachel yelled in thought-speak directed only at us.

Cassie was farthest from the door. But in two more steps Visser Three would see her.

<Remorphing!> Cassie said. <But —>
<Distraction!> Prince Jake yelled.

Hoo-hoo-hoo! E-YAH! E-YAH!

We started screeching, but the Visser was indifferent. We were caged. We were an inferior species. The great Yeerk Visser was uninterested in us. In fact, he seemed bored. Like he was performing some tedious duty.

Of course! It was just a routine inspection. Only by monumental misfortune had we encountered him. And in two seconds that misfortune would turn fatal. We were caged! Helpless!

<Poop him!> Marco yelled suddenly.

<What?>

Marco swept his hand across the bottom of his dirty cage. He grabbed a handful of . . . well, of dung.

A swift, overhand throw. The . . . product . . . flew!

It hit Visser Three full in his face.

<Poop him!> Marco yelled again.

I swept my big chimpanzee hand across the cage floor and without pause threw the . . . items . . . as hard as I could, and with as great an accuracy as I could.

The result was that a large glop stuck on Visser Three's right stalk eye.

<Yah HAH!> I cried in sheer glee.

It was an unusual tactic. A desperate tactic. But I must say it was truly satisfying.

CHAPTER 11

The six of us hurled biological waste product. Then the genuine chimpanzees, sensing a game, joined in.

The air filled with product.

Visser Three was covered within seconds. So were his human-Controller assistants. The four of them beat a hasty retreat through the doorway.

<Now *that* was fun!> Rachel said happily.

Cassie was fully chimpanzee again.

The tactic had succeeded brilliantly.

Then, from beyond the door, came the thought-speak sound of Visser Three's rage.

<Kill them all!>

I shot a look at Prince Jake.

One of the human-Controllers must have argued with the Visser.

WHAM!

The door blew open. A human-Controller landed on the floor. One of his hands had been reduced to a stump. The hand itself lay nearby.

<I don't care if they're test animals!> Visser Three raged. His voice lowered to a sinister, insinuating, false-friendly tone. <I'm here to close this facility, anyway. Phase Two is already a success. This series of tests has been superseded.>

"Y-y-y-yes, Visser!"

<So I want them all killed! Do you understand me?> he said calmly.

"Y-yes! Yes! Yes, Visser!"

<What? No argument? You don't want to question my orders?> the Visser asked pleasantly. He arched his tail forward and almost caressed the human-Controller's neck with the blade.

"NO! No, Visser Three. Never!"

The Visser withdrew his tail. He bent over and picked up the human-Controller's severed hand. He looked at it with interest and then tossed it to the injured man. <Here. Reattach it. And destroy these creatures.> He turned and stalked away, but then stopped. <Bring the Taxxons in from the control room. No point wasting fresh meat.>

61

Visser Three disappeared. One human-Controller was holding his own hand. The other two were very pale.

Visser Three is not a leader who believes it is important to be popular with subordinates.

CHAPTER 12

<That's our signal to get *outta* here,> Marco said.

The human-Controllers left the room, practically knocking one another over in their haste to obey Visser Three's orders.

<Demorph!> Prince Jake said. <Fast!>

No one needed to be told twice. The Taxxons would not take long to arrive.

I demorphed to Andalite. Cassie was already human. She kept morphing. Maybe a fly, maybe a flea, I could not be sure. I saw antennae. I saw bizarre mouth-parts. But mostly, I saw her shrink. She kept morphing only long enough to be able to squeeze between the bars.

Once out and free, she stopped her morph

and quickly returned to human. She grabbed the keys and with quick, trembling hands released one Andalite and three humans. Tobias was hawk again and simply walked through the bars.

Cassie began to open the other chimpanzee cages.

"What are you doing?" Marco asked her.

"I'm letting them out. You heard what Visser Three said. They're going to be killed."

"All we have to do is morph to flies and go out through the door," Marco said. "Once the Taxxons get here . . . I mean, no one is going to count the chimps. But if they get here and find nothing to eat, the Yeerks are going to realize they've been had. They're going to know we were here."

"You guys can go," Cassie said. Her eyes flashed. Her jaw muscles worked. They are signs of determination in humans.

"Marco's right," Prince Jake said. "We can make a clean getaway. If they realize we've been here, they'll be on guard at the meatpacking plant. It'll make it harder for us."

"Not if we stick to chimpanzee morph," Cassie argued. "Yeah, if we went to grizzly bear and tiger and all. But what if we only do chimpanzees?"

I looked at Rachel. She smiled. "I'm in."

"You always back Cassie," Marco said angrily.

Rachel shook her head. "Nah. I just like the idea of the chimpanzees getting some back, you know?"

Cassie was already halfway into chimpanzee morph. Rachel was following. I waited to see what Prince Jake would do.

"So much for me being in charge," Prince Jake muttered. Then he began to morph.

We had just all made it into chimpanzee morph when the door opened and the first Taxxon pushed his slithering bulk into the room. The needle-sharp rows of legs skittered on the tiles. The round, red mouths gaped. The row of jelly eyes glittered.

There is an Earth animal called a centipede. It is similar to a Taxxon, although a hundredth the size. And I do not believe centipedes are cannibalistic.

A Taxxon's hunger is so great, so overpowering, that even the Yeerk in a Taxxon's head cannot control it. A Taxxon will eat any living thing. Including another Taxxon.

Taxxons are cruel but not strong. Perhaps they would have been able to attack and kill disunited, essentially peaceful chimpanzees.

But what they faced were not chimpanzees. They faced chimpanzees animated by the will of

65

their much more intelligent and much more violent cousins: Homo sapiens.

What awaited the Taxxons were creatures with all the tremendous strength and agility of the chimpanzee, united with all the war-making skill of humans.

"Srreeeee!" the Taxxons cried, in giddy anticipation of a meal.

"Hoo-Hoo-Hoo!" the genuine chimpanzees cried, and retreated to their cages.

But six of the chimpanzees waited calmly. They had armed themselves with a variety of weapons: a screwdriver, a chair, a computer monitor.

The lead Taxxon reared up, ready to slam its upper third down on us.

<You know, I *really*, *really* hate Taxxons,> Rachel said.

I stepped in swiftly and struck straight up with a wrench I had discovered. The Taxxon's soft underbelly opened like a moistened paper bag.

Srrr-EEEEEEEEEE!

Rachel moved fast. She rolled in beneath the Taxxon and yanked off one of its sharp legs. Now she had a weapon.

The lead Taxxon motored its dozens of legs and tried to scramble back.

Too late. It had been injured. Its blood was flowing.

The other Taxxons surged into the cramped space and attacked their fellow creature. The Yeerks in their heads were no doubt doing all in their power to stop the cannibalistic massacre.

But nothing can control a Taxxon's hunger.

Prince Jake grabbed the exterior door — the one that led out to the truck. But the door was locked from outside.

We had only one other choice.

<Let's bail!> Tobias said. <Right over them! Into the lab!>

CHAPTER 13

We escaped. The genuine chimpanzees followed us. For a while. But they proved impossible to organize. Cassie did all she could. We all did. But the chimpanzees, while intelligent by the standards of nonhuman animals, are still limited.

Too limited even to grasp their own freedom.

As we raced and bounded and swung through the lab, the true chimpanzees split off, preoccupied with bright lights and shiny objects.

How can I describe what we saw as we raced through room after room looking for an exit? Chimpanzees were not the only creatures being used for experimentation.

There were smaller monkeys. Rats. Dogs.

I soon saw why humans prefer to draw an arbitrary line between themselves and other animals. Had humans been used as these animals were used, the only appropriate descriptive word would have been torture.

Torture.

Useful, no doubt. Medically justifiable, most likely. And it is not my business to judge humans. But this behavior of theirs did trouble me.

After dark that night, I ran into the open fields to feed. The night was black. Even the lights from the neighborhood where the others lived seemed dim. Earth's single moon was only a sliver in the sky. It was a visible difference between Earth and my home world. But I was finding that the differences I could not see mattered much more.

Andalite creatures live in greater harmony than Earth animals. I thought of the *kafit* birds, the *hoobers*, and the *djabalas*. We practiced morphing these creatures, but caging them, killing them, eating them was unthinkable. We were creatures of the same world.

But as Marco, or perhaps Rachel, had once said: Earth is a tough neighborhood. The competition for survival on Earth is brutal. This is a planet filled with powerful, violent predators.

Predators armed with huge teeth, impervious armor, claws that could open an Andalite's body from end to end.

And yet it is Homo sapiens, with his weak jaw and purely symbolic claws, with his soft, unarmored flesh, who rules.

For millions of years we Andalites have not felt the pressure from other species. With our speed and our tails we are without physical peers on our home world. It is different for humans. There are parts of this planet where even today humans are prey to stronger animals.

Perhaps that explains the odd, disconnected human attitudes toward other Earth species. Some they cherish and pamper. Some they protect. Others they use. Still others are annihilated.

And yet would it not seem that they would eat the animals that threatened humans, and not the utterly inoffensive creatures like cows? We certainly didn't choose such animals for battle morphs.

And to abuse chimpanzees, animals almost identical to Homo sapiens, comes very near to a Taxxon view of morality.

<You are an alien,> I reminded myself. <And furthermore, you are a grazer by nature. Not a predator.>

I was perhaps not the person to fairly judge human habits. My understanding of human evolution was that it began with hunter-gatherers. Humans never had the option of simply grazing.

When I got back to the scoop, I turned on my TV after making a few adjustments. I stood close to change the channels, watching as colors and figures flashed by. A woman singing. A newscaster intoning that several local people had been reported missing. Teeth, and toothpaste. A cheeseburger. It looked delicious.

I turned the set off.

Wings rustled above me. Tobias was gliding in for a landing, his talons clutching a black plastic rectangle. He released it as he swept his wings forward to clutch the nearest branch.

<A present for you, Ax-man.>

I picked it up. Gray buttons in the shapes of numbers and arrows covered one side.

<What is it?>

<It's a universal TV remote. I spotted it in a Dumpster.>

A TV remote? What was remote about it? <Thank you, Tobias. But I do not understand.>

<Turn the TV on.> He opened his wings and swooped down from the branch. <You use it to change channels. You know, so you don't have to get off the sofa. Or, well, the ground.>

I switched on the TV and sat back in the scoop, too far to reach the set. I pointed and pushed the "up" arrow.

Images blurred and noises blended together as the remote changed the channels. Marvelous! Much more efficient! I would expend fewer calories per channel changed. When I realized the time I could save . . .

<Oh, look! It is *Friends*!>

<Just a rerun. Um, Ax?> Tobias cocked his sleek head at me. <How did you get so many channels? I could swear I saw MTV and CNN just now. But you don't have cable, so . . .>

I glanced up from the TV set. Phoebe was playing her guitar at Central Perk. <I made improvements.>

Tobias hopped close to the set and peeked behind it. <Oh, man. What is all this?>

<A primitive satellite receiver.>

<You made a satellite dish out of a broken radio, two old soda cans, and . . . what is this?> He held a piece of thick black wire in his beak.

<The wire that humans hang from limbless trees. Very convenient. I found it this evening before I fed.>

Tobias quickly dropped it. <Ah. That would explain the power outage in Jake's neighborhood.>

<Power outage?> I was shocked. <That black wire controls the electric power?>

<When it's not stolen for personal use, yeah.>

<Ridiculous. Why is it not better protected? And why should one small piece matter? The management of your power sources is quite primitive.>

Friends was over. But I was happy to try the remote again.

<Ax, stop! Go back!> Tobias jerked his head at the TV. I flicked back to the previous channel.

". . . no one was injured," a blond woman said. Behind her a small box showed a picture of a chimp being wrestled into a cage. "The chimpanzees were finally captured shortly after six, although traffic on Broad Street was tied up for two hours while animal handlers from The Gardens attempted to catch them."

<The chimps from the truck,> Tobias said.

<The ones we freed.> I nodded.

"No one has reported the chimps missing, but there has been a lot of speculation about where the chimps might have come from," the woman continued. "One eyewitness reported seeing them jump from the back of a truck, but that truck has not been found."

Tobias and I looked at each other. I turned the TV off.

<Well, at least those chimps will have better lives,> Tobias said.

<Yes.> I hesitated. <Humans are inconsistent.>

<Yeah. They are. We are. But you know what? We have to spend tomorrow observing a slaughterhouse. So how about we just chill? Let's watch a sitcom.>

I nodded, a habit I have picked up from humans. <And some of *These Messages*.>

CHAPTER 14

Once again, while the others were in school learning history, mouth sounds, the simpler forms of mathematics, and largely incorrect science, Tobias and I flew in the skies above the meatpacking plant.

It was a rainy day, which made for difficult, unpleasant flying. And what we were required to observe was even more unpleasant.

We met the others in Cassie's barn after they returned from school. Cassie was already at work, tending to the various sick and injured animals. Prince Jake helped her to move several cages.

Rachel flipped through a catalog. A brief book that shows humans what types of artificial skin to acquire.

Marco was working on "homework." He looked up at Prince Jake. "Hey! Is it Molotov and von Ribbentrop or von Molotov and Ribbentrop? Or are they both von?"

"Neither," Rachel said seriously. "It's von Damme and von Halen."

"That's very funny, Rachel. Hah. Hah. And also . . . Hah. But what I have here is a makeup paper cubed. It's a makeup paper for the makeup paper I was supposed to do for my first makeup paper."

"Okay, what did you guys find?" Prince Jake asked Tobias and me.

Tobias was in the rafters, his usual place. <There's no "u" in "Soviet,"> he said to Marco.

Marco crossed out the word and wrote it again.

To everyone, Tobias said, <Well, we found your basic meatpacking plant. Cows go in one end, hamburger comes out the other end.>

<I believe they are called steer,> I interrupted. <Male cows are bulls unless they have been neutered, in which case they are steer. Steer are more docile. Although this herd comprises both steer and cows.>

Everyone except Tobias stared at me.

"Say what?"

<I saw it on the Animal Planet channel,> I explained. <But what is neutering?>

"Oooh! I don't get that channel," Cassie said. "Ax, do you think . . ."

"Moving right along . . ." Marco said, and crossed his legs.

<One big problem,> Tobias said. <There's no force field over the meatpacking plant —>

<It is too large an area,> I explained. <As you know, energy expenditure for a force field increases exponentially. To put it in simple terms, if a field containing ten thousand of your cubic feet uses energy denoted as x, a field containing twenty thousand of your cubic feet will not use $2x$, but rather x cubed.>

"Hey!" Cassie said in alarm. "I actually understood that. I never understand his technical explanations. What's happening to me?"

I was pleased by my success at reducing a much more complex reality to terms simple enough for my human friends to grasp.

"No force field, that's good. So what's the problem?" Prince Jake asked Tobias.

I answered. <Gleet BioFilters at all entrances to the meatpacking plant. As you recall, the Yeerks now use Gleet BioFilters at the entrance to Yeerk pools. They are programmed to destroy any DNA pattern other than those programmed in. At the meatpacking plant those filters eliminate all but steer and humans.>

<We saw a lot of flies get fried,> Tobias said.

"So if we go in, we go in as cows?" Marco said. "*Cows*? In a *slaughterhouse*? Does anyone else see a problem with that? Show of hands: Who would like to be a cow in a meatpacking plant?"

<Big problem number two,> Tobias continued. <The steer are kept somewhere else. A feedlot maybe two miles away. They load 'em into a truck. Which brings us to big problem number three: The cows all have number tags like earrings. They don't just grab a bunch of cows. They grab specific cows.>

"Sure. Inventory," Cassie said. "They need to be able to track back on any health problems."

Honk! Honk! Honk! Honk!

A goose began making loud, distressed noises as Cassie attempted to force a pill into its mouth. "So what do we have? One: We need to acquire specific cows. Two: We need to get their tags off and onto us. Three: We need to get on the truck and travel two miles without having to demorph. Four: We need to get inside the meatpacking plant and avoid being turned into Salisbury steak. Five: We find out what's going on there that has Visser Three so happy and bust it up."

"It all sounds so simple when you put it in that nice one, two, three format," Marco said. "You forgot six: six cows in a meatpacking plant."

<I have seen steer at close range now,> I said. <I do not believe they will be very formidable in combat. The cows even less so.>

Marco pointed at me. "Listen to the man."

"We don't need to all morph cows," Cassie said. "The Gleet BioFilter doesn't eliminate organisms inside of other organisms."

"Do not say the word 'tapeworm,'" Rachel warned.

Cassie laughed. "No tapeworms. Flies. In the cow's nostrils. Maybe two of us morph cows. The others go as flies. In the nostrils."

Now everyone stared at Cassie. Including me.

"So basically, we have a choice. We can go as burgers . . . or boogers," Marco said.

Prince Jake laughed. "Tonight we acquire the cows and get the tags. Tomorrow's Saturday. We do the main action tomorrow A.M. Ax goes as burger. If he has to demorph the Yeerks will see an Andalite, not a human. Tobias is the other one. The rest of us —"

"The rest of us ride the cow booger express," Marco said.

CHAPTER 15

In the afternoon there was a break in the rain. But by the time darkness fell, a new weather front had moved in. Rain and lightning and thunder.

It interfered with my television reception. There was a very simple technological fix for the problem. But I would have to go to the mall. To Radio Shack.

However, there was no time this night.

We flew through the cool, dark, very wet night. I was in owl morph. Owls are wonderful night fliers. But not even an owl enjoys flying through rain.

<Ah, the life of a superhero,> Marco complained. <One big party.>

<We're almost there,> Tobias said.

<Good. I'm almost drowned.>

<What are you complaining about? It's harder for me than it is for you,> Tobias grumbled. <I'm still a hawk. I'm not nocturnal. I'm diurnal.>

<Diurnal? Have you tried Kaopectate?>

<Marco?> Rachel said.

<Yes, Rachel.>

<Shut. Up.>

It was just the four of us. Prince Jake and Cassie had family functions of some sort to deal with. Only Tobias and I were needed to acquire the cows. Marco and Rachel came along for extra security.

That, plus the fact that Rachel was needed to carry a piece of equipment. Her eagle morph is the largest and most powerful of all our bird morphs. But even she could barely lift the small device Cassie had found for us. The device that affixed ear tags.

Owl eyes saw through the darkness like it was day. I could see the raindrops themselves as they fell, sparkling around me. I could see the individual splashes of raindrops hitting cars and slick streets and dripping trees.

I could see humans scurrying from car to doorway, or huddling beneath primitive cover devices called umbrellas.

Humans dislike rain. I believe it is because it

makes the ground slippery. When you are forever teetering wildly on two legs, you resent anything that makes it more difficult to stand.

Every few minutes there would come a huge flash of light. It would illuminate the night with bright blue light and cast deep black shadows. After the flash would, of course, come thunder. Often quite loud. Especially to an owl's sensitive ears.

<That's the feedlot up ahead,> Tobias announced.

My night vision was superior to his, but Tobias has experience at seeing and remembering the world from the air.

<About time,> Rachel grumbled. <I am more than ready to put this stupid ear staple gun down.>

We glided in toward the muddy field. Rachel landed at the first opportunity, dropping the stapler in the mud and coming to rest on a fence. I stayed in the air. I was least tired, being in my natural element, so to speak. And my owl eyes were needed.

We had to spot particular steer from the sequence of numbers that would be called up tomorrow. Preferably the first two numbers in that sequence.

My vision was up to the task. I could see the numbers clearly. But there were a lot of steer and cows in the field. It took some time. I had to stop and demorph and remorph once, well away from the field.

But at last I found them both. They were not too far apart, fortunately.

<Over here, Tobias,> I called. <This brown one.>

<Swell,> he said. He flapped up off the fence and drifted casually over to the steer. He landed directly on the animal's back. The steer flicked its tail. It turned its big head to look back and see what had landed on its rear. Then it went on chewing its cud.

<That was easy,> Tobias said a moment later. <I am cow-capable.>

It was less easy for me. You can only acquire an animal's DNA when you are in your normal body. That meant I had to touch the steer as an Andalite.

I thought perhaps the steer would not mind my presence. I am, after all, not a predator. I am, like them, a grazing animal. Although I graze quite differently.

<Trouble!> Tobias said suddenly. <Car lights! Coming this way.>

CHAPTER 16

We waited, frozen. My friends peered through the darkness. A bolt of lightning split the sky and illuminated the approaching vehicle.

<That's a pickup truck moving over there,> Marco said. <Looks like it's riding around the various pastures. Or enclosures or whatever.>

<It's so dark, what can they possibly see?> Rachel wondered.

<They could have night-vision glasses,> Marco said. <They could see plenty. Like, say, an Andalite.>

<I believe that if I keep my tail lowered and my arms down by my sides I would look enough like a cow or steer not to be noticed,> I suggested.

<Give it a try,> Rachel said.

I landed near a knot of steer. They were standing around, making lowing sounds from time to time. They were indifferent to the presence of an owl in their midst.

I focused my thoughts on demorphing. Within seconds I was rising from the muddy, cow-feces-strewn ground. Up and up I grew. My feathers gave way to sleek blue fur. My stalk eyes re-emerged, much to my relief. It is wonderful to have an owl's night vision. But nerve-wracking to be unable to see in all directions at once. It's like being half-blind.

For a moment I thought the steer might panic. They did not. However, they did decide to move away from me. I tried to stay with them — not an easy thing to do with two tiny legs sticking out of your chest, and your hind legs nothing but large talons.

I staggered and fell facedown in the mud. Lightning flashed. Thunder exploded. And I heard Marco say, <That truck may be heading this way. Hard to tell. All I see is the headlights.>

I continued demorphing. At this point it was more advisable to complete the morph and become fully Andalite. As an Andalite I might conceivably pass as a steer. But in my present condition I could be nothing but some horrid genetic mutation.

As I picked myself up out of the mud, I, too, could see the headlights illuminating rain that had begun to diminish.

I hugged my arms to my body. I tucked my tail down along my back, which enlarged my profile. I bent my head forward, doing my best to simulate a steer's head. I even twisted my stalks forward to simulate horns.

It was not a bad deception, all in all. I was proud of myself. But also just a bit embarrassed. Steer are clearly not sentient animals. My ability to pass as one merely amused Marco.

<Hey, Ax, why is it when I look at you I start thinking about special sauce, lettuce, cheese, pickles, and onions on a sesame seed bun?>

<Here comes the truck,> Rachel warned. <Look steerlike.>

I did my best. I kept my profile turned to the road. I looked most cowlike from that angle.

Then . . .

<It's stopping!> Rachel cried.

<Ax-man, guys are getting out of the truck!>

<I don't see any weapons,> Marco said tersely. <But . . . well . . . I do see beer bottles.>

<It's a bunch of college kids!>

I could hear loud, almost-hysterical giggles. And now I could see the humans, four of them, attempting to climb the fence into the field. One fell down in the mud. The others all laughed.

<They are faced,> Marco said. <What's this about? These aren't security guys. Not unless the Yeerks have gotten really laid-back.>

The four young males staggered and wallowed and half-crawled out onto the field. One of them made a lunge for a steer. He missed and fell. He lay on his back, unmoving.

The other three headed toward me.

If I moved I would not move like a steer. My best plan would be to remain motionless. The humans were quite likely to pass me by.

But that hope did not last long. The humans came for me. They weaved and wandered, but the essential thrust of their digressions was toward me.

<What should I do?> I asked the others. <Is this an attack?>

<I don't think so,> Tobias said. <In fact, I think I know what they're up to. It's called cow-tipping.>

<Of course!> Marco said. <Cow-tipping. It's like a dumb fraternity thing.>

<Kindly explain this cow-tipping,> I asked.

<Well . . . well, basically you go out in a field and push a cow over.>

<Why?>

<I don't know,> Marco admitted. <But it generally involves being profoundly drunk.>

<Why?>

87

<Because it's too idiotic to do sober,> Rachel said, exasperated. <Perfect! We don't have enough bull to deal with, now we have drunk, stupid frat guys.>

<They will reach me in a few seconds,> I said.

<Use your tail. Cut their heads off,> Rachel said disgustedly. <They'll be no loss. Besides, these jerks are driving.>

<Remove their heads?>

<She's kidding!> Tobias said.

<Perhaps I could so something less drastic,> I suggested.

The three inebriated humans came close and stopped. Even stopped, they continued to move in a weaving, waving pattern, as though they were being blown by a very strong wind.

"That's a weird-looking cow, dude," one of the humans said.

"Cow? That's no cow, man, unless I'm really —"

Fwapp!

Fwapp!

Fwapp!

I snapped my tail three times.

Shlump! Shlump! Shlump!

<What did you do?!> Marco cried.

<I hit them with the flat of my blade,> I explained. <I applied the necessary force to the

sides of their heads. I believe they are unconscious.>

<I believe they'll stay that way for a while,
too,> Rachel said with a laugh. <Okay, Ax. Acquire some beef and let's haul.>

<Yes. I would like to make it home in time to
watch *The Brady Bunch*. It is a story. About a
lovely lady. Who was bringing up three very lovely
girls.>

CHAPTER 17

The next day I performed the morning ritual solemnly. I repeated the words that spoke of freedom, duty, and obedience, spreading my arms and bowing at the appropriate times.

<The destruction of my enemies, my most solemn vow.> I straightened up and assumed the fighting stance.

<I, Aximili-Esgarrouth-Isthill, Andalite warrior-cadet, offer my life.> I drew my tail blade against my throat, then relaxed it. I was done.

As it was designed to do, the ritual gave me strength of purpose that morning. Even here on Earth I was serving my people. Andalites *and* humans.

<Ready?> Tobias asked as he coasted down out of a perfect blue sky. The rain had blown away in the night. The morning was the type of weather that humans consider perfect: warm but not too warm, a few white clouds, but not enough to obscure the sun.

<Yes, I am ready.>

<Maybe I need a morning ritual,> Tobias suggested. <I mean, something beyond passing a pellet and eating a mouse. Something with some meaning.>

<My morning ritual is imposed on me by my society,> I pointed out. <Your society — human society — does not impose a similar requirement.>

<Unless you consider drinking coffee and scarfing a toaster strudel a ritual.>

<I do find the ritual helpful sometimes. On days when I expect to face danger, for example. But it causes me to miss some of the banter between Katie and Matt and Al.>

<Who and who and who?>

<They are the humans who appear regularly on the *Today* show,> I explained.

<Uh-huh. I haven't caught that lately.>

<They are taking an in-depth look at exercises to trim the fat from problem areas such as thighs, upper arms, and hips.>

I began to morph to harrier. Minutes later I was flying.

I fly often. But I have never come to see it as normal. Walking like a human is merely tedious and annoying. But flying like a hawk is the most wonderful experience imaginable.

I opened my wings, flapped them up and down, tucked my talons up beneath me, and spread my tail to increase my lift. Suddenly I was no longer tied to the ground.

We flew along the treetops till we found a thermal. A thermal is a pillar of warm air that rises from heated ground. It fills your wings and lifts you almost effortlessly.

We rose to a hundred feet, high enough to escape the notice of most humans on the ground. And we flew toward a meeting with the others at the feedlot.

It was a much more pleasurable flight than the earlier one. Now I could see to put the feedlot in context. Human habitations tend to cluster in ever-tighter proximity. The tightest clusters are called cities. As one moves out from this tight center, wider spaces appear. These are suburbs. Beyond the suburbs the spaces grow, until soon open fields are more prevalent than dwellings.

According to Marco, this is known as "Gooberville" or "The Middle of Nowhere." The

JOIN THE ANIMORPHS ALLIANCE ®

START THE ADVENTURE WITH

- The first 3 ANIMORPHS books
- ANIMORPHS poster
- Bookends with 4 detachable morphs
- Animorphs*Flash* Newsletter
- Members only Flip/Trivia Book
- The "A" Pendant

Join today!
This introductory pack will arrive at your home about 4 weeks after you fill out and mail the attached order card.

Great Savings!
For as long as you like, you'll continue to receive the next 3 books in the series as well as the members only Animorphs*Flash* newsletter each month for $11.99 (plus shipping and handling). You may cancel anytime.

No risk...
To enjoy this gift-packed, free trial invitation, simply detach, complete with parent's signature, and return the postage-paid FREE Trial Invitation form on the other side.

Respond today!
Offer expires December 31, 1999.

feedlot was at the vague border of the suburbs and Gooberville.

I saw a number of other birds of prey in the sky ahead. They were spread far apart and at different altitudes. I spotted Rachel first, with her huge eagle wingspread. Prince Jake, in his peregrine falcon morph, was the smallest, but also the fastest.

We spiraled down to the field. Our plan was simple. We had used the stapler to remove ear tags from the two relevant steer the night before. We now had the tags. Tobias and I were to morph the steer and Cassie would affix the ear tags. We had left the stapler at the site.

A simple plan.

Or so we thought.

CHAPTER 18

Tobias and I had the easy part, really. We picked out a cluster of steer and landed in the mud between them. The steer showed no interest in us. Prince Jake stayed in the air overhead, keeping watch. Cassie and Rachel and Marco landed in various areas outside the lot, fairly distant from one another so that we didn't look like a suspicious collection of birds of prey.

<Me first,> Tobias said. <That way I can cover you.>

I concentrated on not being trampled by the slow-moving steer as Tobias began his morph.

Morphing is never predictable. It does not always follow a logical course. Different parts morph at different speeds, in different sequences.

In this case, it was the cow head that began to appear first. It was, to say the very least, bizarre. Tobias's short, hooked beak softened and began to extrude. It grew out as it grew flabby. Soon it was nothing more than loose flaps of unsupported skin. The skin was still covered with brown feathers.

Tobias's own furious hawk eyes widened and rounded and seemed to fill with moisture. They no longer looked fierce. They looked . . . well, stupid.

He began to grow all over, but still the feathers persisted for a long time, only melting into short brown fur at the last moment.

His hooves appeared, almost complete, at the end of his tiny hawk legs. His wing tips began to curl and harden and form hooves as well. Only then did his wings stretch into steer legs.

But at last he was fully formed. Fully formed and quite large. And seemingly agitated.

<Tobias? You are in danger of stepping on me.>

<Sorry . . . I . . . I don't know, I just feel kind of antsy, you know? Restless. Like I'm annoyed. Like I'm looking for trouble.>

95

<Are you finding the steer instincts difficult to control?> I asked.

<Not difficult. Just caught me by surprise. I assumed steer morph would be pretty laid-back. Anyway . . . your turn.>

Of course, I had two changes to make, not one. First I had to demorph to Andalite. Once again, the steer began to move away, depriving me of cover. But Tobias snorted at them and took a little trot around the edge of the knot of steer. After that they stayed still.

It was odd. It was as if the steer were afraid of Tobias. Or at least deferential. It should have been a clue that we had a problem. But I was insufficiently familiar with cows and steer to realize what had happened.

<Truck's coming,> Jake reported. <Still on the main road, but let's pick it up.>

Cassie began crossing the field toward us. This was dangerous, of course. Humans are expected to wear certain artificial skin for certain occasions. And Cassie's morphing suit was not appropriate for this occasion. She was barefoot and wearing only a simple but brightly colored skintight "outfit."

"Barefoot black chick in Day-Glo spandex stomping through the cow pies," Cassie had said. "That'll be real smooth."

I became fully Andalite, keeping my upper body ducked down behind Tobias's bulk.

The change was far less severe than many I have endured. I began with four hooved legs, and I ended with four hooved legs. I doubled, if not tripled, in weight, but my basic body configuration was not radically altered.

There were still changes, though. A cow tail is not at all like an Andalite tail. A cow tail is no danger to anyone.

And of course, my arms disappeared, shriveling and withering until they seemed to suck into my body.

I acquired a mouth. A very large mouth. And very large nostrils. And big, vacuous, moist, dark eyes.

There was nothing exceptional about the steer senses. Its sense of smell was good, but, from what I understand, nothing like the intensity of a canine's sense of smell. Its hearing and sight were fair, but less acute than a human's.

The single oddest fact was that my eyes were separated by an enormous face that dominated my field of vision. I could see to the left and to the right. But most of "straight ahead" was filled with my own long muzzle.

But Tobias was wrong. There was nothing agitated or restless about this morph. On the contrary it was very —

<Um . . . Ax-man? I think you messed up. You're a cow.>

<No, I am a steer.>

<No, you're a cow. You have an udder. You acquired the wrong kind of cow!>

<Oh.>

I demorphed. I acquired a steer. This time I checked. I morphed again.

And now I learned Tobias had been correct. The steer's mind was not docile. Not passive. In fact . . . I was angry. And with very good reason: There was a bull nearby.

There was also a human, but she did not matter.

I glared at the bull.

He glared at me.

I snorted and pawed the ground.

It was like watching myself in a mirror. The bull did the same.

It was unavoidable. This pasture only had room for one of us. I would have to attack him and force him to run away.

<Cassie!> I heard Prince Jake call down from high above. <They look like they're squaring off to fight.>

"Uh-oh," Cassie said.

CHAPTER 19

"**A**x! Tobias!" Cassie hissed. "Chill!"

The short human girl kept moving toward us, positioning herself between me and the bull.

And now it occurred to me that maybe I should charge her, too.

"Nice cows. Good cows. Gooooood cows," Cassie said in a strangely soothing voice. "Listen to me, guys. We overlooked a little something. You're not steer. You're bulls."

Prince Jake plummeted, then swooped a few feet off the ground, circled, and came back toward us.

<They look different than the other steer,> he said.

"They are," Cassie said in her sweet, soft,

99

talking-to-dangerous-animals voice. "We kind of forgot something. We kind of forgot that you get to be a nice, docile steer by being neutered. But your DNA is still bull DNA."

<Oh. That's what's different,> Prince Jake said.

What were they talking about? Confusing. Distracting. But the other bull was still there. Still in my pasture. I snorted. He snorted.

I could feel energy quivering through me. I was alive! Ready to charge. Ready to lower my head, dig in my hooves, and launch myself head-long.

"Boys. Ax. Tobias. Listen to me. You are not steer. You are bulls. Bulls are very territorial. You want to fight right now. But that would be a bad idea. A very bad idea."

Prince Jake had swept past and soared back up into the sky. <Cassie! The truck's on the move!>

Cassie nodded. "Okay, it's time for peace here. Arabs and Israelis. Americans and Russians. We do this by stages."

I heard her. I understood her. But I was not interested. I was interested in the fact, the OVERWHELMING fact that there was a bull right in front of me, defying me!

"Ax. Tobias. Each of you take one step back."

<Cassie, you may need to bail!>

Cassie shook her head impatiently. "Come on, good boys, good bulls, one step back. Come on . . . one step back. One step back."

<They're going to spot you, Cassie! Too late to get away. You need to drop and morph!>

"Ax? Tobias?" Cassie said sweetly, calmly, pleasantly. "I . . . said . . . BACK UP!"

The other bull and I both jerked straight back.

<Okay, Rachel, Marco, get ready! This is going to be close.>

Cassie grabbed my horns in her hands and stared right into one of my eyes. "I don't have time for this crap. We have enough trouble. Get control. Do it now." She whipped up her hand-held stapler. She poked the ear tag into the end of the gun and I heard a loud click in my ear. There was a slight, distant sensation of being stuck with something sharp.

Then she swung around and grabbed Tobias the same way. Within seconds we were both tagged. And both able to accept the other's existence.

Almost.

Prince Jake dropped from the sky again. He landed, as Tobias and I had done earlier, between steer. <Cassie! Morph! Those guys are here.>

"We have a problem here," Cassie said. "They aren't exactly steer."

<Do you think the truck drivers will notice?>

"Excuse me? Of course they'll notice! They may be Controllers, but their human hosts are most likely farm folk."

<What do we do? Don't they ever send bulls to the slaughterhouse?>

"Yeah. They do, so maybe if we get there we're okay. But how do we get past these guys in the truck? They'll call in to be sure they're supposed to carry bulls. They'll be mad because bulls are dangerous. They'll realize something is wrong. Ear tag or no ear tag."

<We've gone to too much trouble,> Prince Jake said bitterly. <I don't just want to give up.>

For a long moment no one moved, and no one said anything. Then Prince Jake said something that even I found frightening.

<Marco? Think you can drive their truck?>

CHAPTER 20

The truck came. It rolled right out into the mud. Two humans climbed down.

"Hey! That's no steer," the driver said.

His partner nodded. "That sure ain't no steer."

<And I'm definitely not a steer,> Marco said. He stood up from behind the camouflage provided by Tobias and me.

"That's a gorilla!"

"Fool! It's an Andalite in morph!"

The two men turned to run. They did not get far. At last I had a target for my bull aggression.

I loped easily after them. I lowered my head, aligned my curved horns, and struck one, and then the other in the area humans refer to as "the butt."

They flew several feet and landed on their faces. Marco yanked them up out of the mud.

<Go to sleep,> Marco said as he butted their heads together.

The humans were rendered unconscious.

<How do we make sure they stay out long enough?>

<Take their clothes. That'll slow them down,> Prince Jake said. <I'll demorph. I'm biggest. I should look okay in that guy's jeans and jacket. Marco drives . . .>

<How come Marco drives?> Rachel demanded.

<He has experience.>

"Oh, man, don't even mention that," Cassie said. "My dad cried over the twisted remains of that truck."

<I'll ride shotgun and carry the guy's clipboard,> Prince Jake continued. <Tobias and Ax? See what you can do to persuade some of these steer to get aboard the truck.>

That part proved easy. The steer were nervous about Tobias and me. They were quite content to move away from us, even if that meant climbing a ramp into the back of a truck.

Tobias and I entered last. Cassie and Rachel morphed to flies and made their bobbling, erratic way to perches in our noses. Rachel was with Tobias, Cassie with me.

Marco squeezed his huge gorilla bulk into a denim jacket and pants. Shoes were, of course, an impossibility, given the size of his feet.

Jake's own artificial skin was overly large. But he, at least, was human. He donned a hat — a head covering — and pulled it low to obscure his features.

<Oh yeah, this'll work,> Rachel said in that tone I recognized as sarcasm. <A gorilla wearing some hideous Levi's leisure suit and a kid who looks like he's wearing his dad's clothes, delivering a pair of bulls to a Yeerk meatpacking plant. Nothing weird there.>

<He has to go in gorilla morph,> Cassie said. <The seat's jammed back and he can't reach the pedals.>

<Everyone ready?> Marco asked brightly. <Everyone have a seat belt on? Anyone have to pee before we leave? Go now. I'm not going to stop at every Stuckeys we pass.>

I felt a sudden lurch. The truck moved. Backward. Then stopped. A second lurch. The engine roared but the truck did not move. The sound I heard suggested metal grinding on metal.

<Oh yeah,> Marco said. <Clutch. Forgot about that. I mean, who has a standard transmission nowadays?>

Prince Jake must have said something. Because then Marco said, <Hey, no one is going to

105

die on the way there. I'll get us all there. Everyone will still be available to die when we get there.>

<That's comforting,> Tobias grumbled.

More loud grinding. Suddenly we were propelled forward. All the steer staggered. We lurched and rolled across the field and Marco said, <Hah! See? No problemo.>

<Let's see how you do out on the road,> Tobias said.

I heard a loud crunching sound. <What was that?> I asked.

<Fence,> Marco said.

A few seconds later, a very similar sound.

<More fence, okay?> Marco said. <Everyone just shut up, I have it under control.>

Off we went, down the road. I had a very limited exterior view out of the right-hand side. I saw trees flash by. I saw more fields with more cows. I saw a pickup truck, with its horn blaring and its driver forming a sort of salute with one raised finger.

It occurred to me that oncoming vehicles should not be passing by on the right.

<Hey, that guy gave me the finger!>

<Some people take it personally when you nearly run them down,> Tobias said. <Some people have no sense of humor.>

I could see the long, low building that was the meatpacking plant. We were getting close. I felt a rush of excitement.

<Almost there,> Marco reported. <There's the road. Just need to turn . . . Just need to . . .>

Suddenly the truck swerved wildly. I — and every other animal in the back — fell left.

Thousands of pounds of steer weight had just shifted to the left side of the truck. Just as the truck was teetering left, anyway.

<Ahhhh!> Marco cried.

CHAPTER 21

<Aaaahhhhh!>

The truck was no longer moving on multiple wheels arrayed along both sides. It was crazily tipped to the left, moving solely on the wheels of one side.

<Aaaaahhhhh!>

Bull and steer, we were all shoved to one side, piled against one another. The floor of the truck bed tilted up and away at an absurd angle.

We were going to tip over!

And yet . . . the truck kept moving. On the wheels of one side, tilted almost on its side, it kept moving!

And slowly . . . slowly . . . so . . . slowly . . .

the angle diminished. We tilted back to the right. Then . . .

WHAM!

The truck settled back onto all its wheels.

THUMP THUMP THUMP THUMP

The steer, Tobias, and I all fell over to the right. The truck now tilted to the right, but not nearly as far.

WHAM!

The truck settled again, and we blew down the road toward the meatpacking plant.

<Bond,> Marco said. <James Bond.>

Scrrrrreeeeeee!

Marco hit the brakes and the truck came slithering and fishtailing to a stop at the gate of the meatpacking plant.

Now that the cargo had been reshuffled, I had a better, clearer view out the left side of the truck. I could see two armed guards approaching the cab. They seemed somewhat disturbed. Possibly awed. Possibly admiring. Possibly frightened.

It is sometimes hard to decipher human facial expressions.

"What are you, *crazy*?" one guard shouted.

"Bad shocks, man," Marco said in a low, gutteral, muddy voice.

I was startled to hear him make mouth

sounds. He must have partially demorphed to human. Just human enough to pass.

"Bad shocks! What are you, nuts? You should be locked up! You should be in a rubber room!"

"Here, just sign off on the manifest," Prince Jake said, trying to lower his own voice.

"You're cleared," the second guard said. "Just let us know when you're gonna leave, so we can stay out of your way."

<Oh goody, they're letting us in,> Tobias said darkly.

Marco segued back into gorilla morph as soon as the guards stepped back. <I think I see a ramp up there. That must be where we go,> he said. Then, in obvious reply to Prince Jake, <Sure, I can back up to the ramp. Why wouldn't I be able to back up?>

<Oh, man, this is going to be ugly,> Rachel said, speaking from Tobias's nostril.

The truck jerked forward, stopped. Jerked forward again. Stopped. *Grind!* Lurched into reverse. Stopped. *Grind!* Lurched. Stopped. Forward. Lurch. Backward. Stop. *Grind!* Lurch. Forward. Stop.

<I've heard of a three-point turn,> Cassie said. <I guess this would be the thirty-point turn.>

Lurch. Backward.
WHAM!

Every steer lurched backward with the impact.

<All right, we're there,> Marco announced.

<These cows are going to be looking forward to a nice, easy death after this ride,> Rachel said.

<Tobias? Sneeze and blow Rachel a few hundred feet.>

I saw a large man jump down off the platform and come running around to the front of the truck. He was yelling. "Where did you learn how to drive, you moron? I'm gonna kick . . . hey! Where's the driver?"

<We've morphed to flies,> Prince Jake informed us. <Coming back around.>

<I can't tell one gigantic planet-sized cow from the next,> Marco said.

<Tobias and Ax? Toss your heads a little. We want the right nostril.>

With a startlingly loud noise, the back gate of the truck swung open. The large man and a very thin man were conferring.

"I have never seen driving like that! No wonder the driver took off. He must have been drunk. He must be a lunatic!"

"Hey! Those are bulls!"

"Well, I'll be a . . . transported like this? This really is nuts!"

The skinny man narrowed his eyes suspiciously. "Andalite bandits?"

The large man laughed. "I think an Andalite could figure out how to drive a truck. Besides, even an Andalite isn't stupid enough to morph a steer or even a bull and walk into a slaughter-house. They'd have to be idiots."

<Could not have said it better myself,> Marco muttered.

From the building, awful smells reached my nostrils: blood. Manure. Blood. Biological rot. And more blood.

And more blood.

CHAPTER 22

Down a narrow chute we went. Three steers moved ahead. Then me. Tobias was behind me.

Over the mouth of the chute was an arch. The Gleet BioFilter.

The first steer reached it. I saw a flash of light, followed by a faint sizzling sound. I could not see them from this angle, but I was sure a number of fleas, flies, lice, and assorted other small creatures had been killed.

<Get as far into our nostrils as you can,> I instructed my friends in fly morph.

<I'm in so far I can see your brain,> Marco said.

<That is highly unlikely.>

I reached the BioFilter. I felt a slight tingle, like static electricity. Then I was through.

<Marco? Cassie?>

<We're fine,> Cassie said. <But it's good to get deep. I saw a real fly get zapped for being too close to the outside.>

<We're still here, enjoying our little field trip in Cow Nose Caverns,> Marco reported.

<Okay, everyone get ready,> Prince Jake said. <This isn't going to be pretty if we're too slow.>

A moment later, Rachel reported, <We're through!>

<Hit it!> Jake said.

I felt a tickle as Marco and Cassie exited from my nostrils. Four nearly invisible flies disappeared quickly from view. Leaving Tobias and me alone.

Very, very alone.

<So,> Tobias said. <Seen anything good on TV lately?>

<Are you attempting to distract us from our fear by engaging in irrelevant conversation?>

<Yeah.>

<In that case, I did enjoy watching *The Simpsons*. I assume that they do not represent some variant species of humans but are in fact humorous pictorial exaggerations of humans?>

<Yeah. They're cartoons.>

<Cartoons, yes. They seemed to be related to

humans but lacked a sufficient number of fin-gers.>

<Oh, God!>

<What?>

<Look! Look!>

I looked up. I could not see directly in front of me because other cattle were blocking my view. But as the chute turned a corner I saw a horrific vision: dozens of cows hanging by their rear legs. They seemed almost to be flying. Flying as they were carried along by an overhead conveyor belt.

Flying and no longer alive.

It was a bewildering scene. A confusing as-sembly line, full of separate events and actions.

Cows are not highly intelligent animals. An in-telligent animal, smelling the blood, catching this brief glimpse of the future, would have bolted, kicked, fought.

But no, maybe that is not true, either. Maybe an intelligent animal would understand that it was doomed and attempt to face the inevitable calmly.

In any event, neither Tobias nor I were cows. And neither of us was intellectually impaired.

<Forget this!> Tobias said.

<We must wait for the others to return,> I managed to say.

One noise was louder than the others. And getting nearer all the time. It was straight ahead.

I craned my neck. I was taller than the steer ahead of me.

I looked past him, and at first did not understand what I was seeing. The lead steer came up to a place where pneumatic forces pushed the sides of the chute in, locking the animal in place.

A man, acting with practiced ease, whipped shackles around the back legs.

A second man held a large tool against the head of the steer. The tool had a cylinder on top.

He squeezed a trigger.

BANG!

The tool jerked. The steer fell. In its forehead was a hole.

Instantly it was jerked into the air by its legs.

I counted two more steer between me and the killing gun.

I have faced death in battle. But never as a dumb beast going to slaughter.

<I have changed my mind,> I said. <Let's get out of here.>

CHAPTER 23

I began to demorph.

No time!

BANG!

Another steer died.

I refused to move forward.

"What do they expect, sending bulls?" a man grumbled. He stepped over to me. He was carrying a tube with two small prongs on the end. He jammed the tube a —

Zzzzapppp!

<Aarrgghh!>

The pain was incredible. I moved forward without intending to. Closer!

I had stopped demorphing.

<Morph!> I screamed at myself.

BANG!

The last steer ahead of me died.

I resisted again. No! No! No!

I dug in my hooves. But now I was demorphing, and from the big bull hooves my own more delicate hooves were emerging. I could barely support my own weight. The man with the shackles would see that . . .

But it would be too late!

Zzzzaaapppp!

Zzzzaaapppp!

The man with the stick rammed it twice. Once in my rump. Then low, under my belly.

The pain!

<Ax!> Tobias cried.

I staggered. But I staggered . . . forward!

My head was clearing slowly.

Fooosh!

The sides of the chute pressed in, holding me tight, immobile.

Morph! Morph! Morph!

<Ax!> Tobias cried. <Ax! AX!>

My eyes watered. My head was swimming. I was confused, lost, dazed.

I looked to my right. The tool was coming for me. Coming straight toward me. I could see the man's finger on the trigger.

Then . . . a new form. Large . . . brown . . . looming up behind the man . . .

<Hey, buddy! Take the rest of the day off,> Rachel said. She swung one massive grizzly bear paw.

The man with the killing tool dropped like one of the steer.

<Cutting it kind of close, aren't you?!> Tobias demanded angrily.

<Sorry,> Rachel said.

I realized I was shaking. Trembling.

Other humans were running now. Many running away. Some running toward us. Toward the bear.

I could not stop trembling. Could not stop the shaking. I was demorphing and shaking.

But even so, I noted the humans who were heading toward the bear, not away.

Controllers, of course. Normal humans would seek to escape. The Controllers among them knew the significance of the bear. They knew — or *thought* they knew — that it was an Andalite in morph.

Dozens left their stations, grabbed long knives, grabbed powered saws, and came for us.

<So much for anything subtle,> Rachel said. <It's going to get hairy.>

She grabbed the sides of the chute with her two front paws and pulled. The wood ripped away easily. I pushed through and out and away.

And just then, my own stalk eyes began to

119

function and I could look back and see my own tail. My own fast, deadly, accurate tail.

I was a grazing animal, like the ones who were fed to this killing place. But I was not a cow.

<Watch out, that guy has a chain saw!> Tobias yelled.

A human-Controller rushed at me with a long, powered saw. The saw screamed.

FWAPP!

Now the human-Controller screamed.

<He no longer has a chain saw,> I said.

CHAPTER 24

<Come on, follow me,> Rachel said. <The others are in trouble. I just came to get you guys.>

<Well, there was no need to rush,> Tobias said. <You could have waited, oh, about another millisecond!>

<Hey, I said I was sorry.>

<Which way?> Tobias demanded.

<Far corner, over there,> Rachel said. <Go! Ax and I will catch up.>

Tobias was hawk once more. He flapped and took off, swerving and dodging through skinned, gutted carcasses. Rachel and I took the slower route: through the human-Controllers and their knives.

We try never to kill any Controller. And humans, in particular, since my human friends have a certain sentimental fondness for others of their own species.

So we were careful. We were restrained. I applied my tail blade with restraint.

But it was difficult. I had been badly frightened. As frightened as I have ever been. And irrational as it might be, I resented the human-Controllers who were even now attempting to butcher me.

We forced our way through the human-Controllers. Forced our way as dripping carcasses floated above us on the conveyor. My hooves scrabbled over spilled entrails.

What we found at the far end of the blood-soaked slaughtering floor was another battle.

Prince Jake in tiger morph. Cassie in wolf morph. Marco in gorilla morph. Tobias, wheeling and plunging to rip and tear.

They were surrounded, cut off, hemmed in by a growing army of human-Controllers.

And worse: Hork-Bajir were pouring into the battle from two directions.

Prince Jake's back was to a closed door. He was roaring and slashing and using his powerful jaws, but the situation was desperate.

They were hemmed in. Cornered. Trapped.

Rachel and I might be able to join them, but then we would be in the same trap.

<Jake! The door behind you!> Rachel cried.

<Can't get it open. We need more muscle! Hurry!>

Rachel turned her huge, shaggy grizzly bear head to me, even as she swatted a human-Controller with a backhand that sent him flying.

<Well, Ax, all we have to do is go through about fifty Hork-Bajir, bust down that door, and find a way out of this hellhole.>

<Yes,> I agreed. <Let us begin.>

Rachel dropped to all fours. She let loose a hoarse roar and charged.

No Andalite accustomed to our more pacific animal life could possibly understand what a grizzly bear charge means. Even most humans would fail to imagine it.

Grizzly bears are not lithe and graceful like the big cats. They are more like dogs. They move with a rolling, lopsided gait that at first seems almost tentative, as if they might stop at any moment.

But then you begin to realize how large they are. And you begin to realize that, awkward or not, they are very fast. And you begin to realize that you are puny, pathetic, weak, and insignificant. You begin to realize that this bear, this rolling, shaggy, unstoppable monster, can kill you from the mere impact of his shoulder hitting you.

I saw all of this on the faces of the human-Controllers before us. Saw their indifference become concern and turn to terror and panic, all in seconds, as Rachel charged.

HHHHHHHROOOOARRRHHHH!

"Run!" many voices agreed.

"Stand fast! Don't run!" one man cried. He planted himself before Rachel. He stood firm. For approximately one and one half seconds.

Then he ran. As Rachel barreled past him he swiped at her with a knife. The knife sliced at fur. He might as well have been swatting at an Andalite Dome ship with a tree branch.

<Rachel! Hork-Bajir!>

Two big Hork-Bajir leaped at her, their arm blades flashing. I whipped my tail left, right. One Hork-Bajir dropped. The other hesitated, just long enough for us to pass him.

We plowed into the defensive knot of our friends.

<On behalf of General Custer, let me welcome you to the last stand,> Marco said as he sank his gorilla fist into the midriff of a Hork-Bajir warrior.

<This the door?> Rachel yelled.

<Yeah! Can you bust it down?>

Rachel reared up on her hind legs. She had to

124

duck her head as split cow carcasses came by, always holding to their stately pace.

She put out her paws and slammed her weight against the door.

WHAM!

Nothing! The door did not budge. And now a triumphant roar went up from the surging, pressing mass of enemy warriors, human and Hork-Bajir.

We were trapped. Outnumbered.

Then we heard the hated thought-speak voice we knew too well.

<How fitting,> Visser Three exulted. <The end of the Andalite bandits comes here in a slaughterhouse. Take them! Seize them! Butcher them! Yes, butcher them!>

CHAPTER 25

<Rachel!> Prince Jake said tersely. <Hit it again!>

WHAM!

Rachel hit the door again. No effect!

Slash!

A Hork-Bajir-blade cut opened right across my chest. Not deep. Not painful. But frightening.

Cassie was covered with matted blood. Marco was using only one arm. The other hung limp. Prince Jake was attacking, attacking, attacking with all the violent ferocity of his tiger morph, but he was tiring. Tobias was having difficulty maneuvering in a "sky" filled with floating cow carcasses.

<Hey! There's a keypad!> Rachel yelled.

126

I turned one stalk eye. There was a keypad. Not a Yeerk design, certainly. Too primitive. But then many of the people working at the facility were not Yeerks.

<Ax!> Jake yelled.

<I will try,> I said. I backed away from the battle, yielding my place to Rachel.

I snapped my tail. My blade shattered the cover of the keypad. I reached in and twisted two wires together.

The door opened.

We plowed through the door. Bloody, exhausted, scared, injured.

Rachel closed the door behind us. I leaped to access the keypad on this side of the door. I ripped out every wire I could reach. Not an elegant solution, but effective.

<Geez, I could have done *that*,> Marco muttered.

A sudden silence descended. Through the door came only muffled sounds of hammering.

<They'll get through before long,> Tobias said.

<Visser Three will pour every Controller he has into this place,> Marco said. <He'll bring them down from orbit. He'll have thousands of them here!>

Only then did we look at the room we had entered.

It was, in most respects, identical to the room at the animal testing laboratory where the chimpanzees had been caged. Rows of cages. Left and right. A concrete floor and white tile walls. Bright lights.

But there was one very significant difference. Where there had been chimpanzees, there were now humans.

Two dozen humans occupied the cages.

They did not move. They did not turn to look at us.

<Are they dead?> Rachel asked.

I said, <No. Bio-stasis, I believe. They can be released from bio-stasis and function normally.>

<What the . . .> Cassie said. Then she reared up on her hind legs and placed her paws against the bars so she could look at a chart on the outside of the nearest cage. <Project Obedience,> she read. <Medication effective.>

She moved to the next cage. <Project Obedience. Medication effective.>

<What medication?> Tobias asked.

<Doesn't say. Just mentions "Formula Seventy-one.">

I spotted a computer console. Definitely Yeerkish in design, quite modern. By Yeerk standards.

It was powered up, open, not protected. Someone had been using it quite recently.

<Project Obedience,> I said to the computer. <Define.>

It replied in a simulated human voice. "Project Obedience is the brilliant insight of our great and glorious leader, Visser Three, hero of the Taxxon rebellion, Scourge of the Andalite fleet, Conqueror of Earth."

<Good grief.> Rachel glanced at the motionless humans in the cages.

"Project Obedience is designed to use genetically engineered biological components to erase those portions of the human brain responsible for free will."

<Say what?> Marco said.

"Project Obedience has successfully tested Formula Seventy-one on chimpanzees, an Earth species related to humans. One hundred percent success has been achieved, thanks to the genius of Visser Three!"

<How exactly do you program a computer to kiss butt like that?> Tobias wondered. He was resting wearily atop one of the cages.

"And human testing has now shown Formula Seventy-one to be one hundred percent effective on humans as well! Phase Three is now ready: The widespread dissemination of Formula Seventy-one through the human food supply, followed by the rapid conquest of planet Earth!"

CHAPTER 26

For a moment no one spoke.

Then Marco said, <They're gonna put some magic formula in meat and it's supposed to take away free will?>

<I believe it is designed to suppress those portions of the human brain responsible for free will,> I said.

<That's insane!>

<If it worked it would allow the Yeerks to take over the entire human race without a fight,> Rachel said.

<Reduce people to mindless automatons,> Prince Jake agreed.

<This is why we're getting killed? Over this?> Cassie demanded.

<What, this isn't serious enough for you?> Marco demanded angrily. <I mean, this could enslave the entire human race within weeks!>

Cassie laughed, almost pityingly. <Oh, please. No way this works.>

<One hundred percent effective,> Prince Jake countered.

<It's a lie,> Cassie said simply.

<You just don't want to face reality,> Rachel said harshly. <I mean, come on! The Yeerks are far more advanced than we are scientifically. They can do this!>

<No,> Cassie said firmly. <They can't. Come on, we should unfreeze, or whatever, these people. We have to free them.>

<You can't free them,> Marco said. <Don't you get it? They've already lost their free will! We unfreeze them, they'll do whatever the Yeerks order them to do. Turn on us! Attack us.>

<We are NOT leaving humans in cages,> Cassie said angrily.

<They're not humans anymore,> Marco raged. <They might as well be Controllers. No free will. Slaves!>

<Now, you listen to me,> Cassie said. <No one, *nothing* can eliminate free will. Don't be ridiculous. Even with a Yeerk in your head, you have free will. Not the will to *do*, but the will to think, to believe, to hope or love or whatever.>

<This is worse than Yeerks, Cassie,> Prince Jake argued. <This goes deeper. One hundred percent effective.>

<I do not wish to interrupt. This is a very interesting discussion,> I said. <However, one question does occur to me.>

<What?> Rachel sighed.

<If these humans have no free will, why are they in cages? And, indeed, why are they being held in bio-stasis?>

A sudden movement. At the far end of the room. A small, older human male wearing spotless white. And holding a Dracon beam.

"D-d-don't move! I'll sh-sh-sh-sh-sh —"

<Shoot,> Rachel supplied. <Don't move or you'll shoot.>

The human nodded. "Get-get-get out of here! Go back out there. You aren't allowed in here!"

<I don't think we can do that,> Prince Jake said calmly. Then, with a movement so swift and fluid that the human did not have time to blink, Prince Jake lunged and knocked the Dracon beam from the man's hand.

The weapon skidded away beneath a cage.

The human reacted strangely.

He began to cry. He collapsed into the chair before the computer console, placed his face in the palms of his hands, and made sounds of crying.

"He'll kill me! Of course, he was going to kill me, anyway. It was only a matter of time."

<"He" being Visser Three, I assume?> I said.

"Of course Visser Three," the man said bitterly. "Who else? This whole project is his idea."

<But it worked. So why would he kill you?> Rachel asked.

The man raised his head and rolled his eyes. "It didn't work. I faked the results. We all did. We had no choice! Visser Three kept demanding results, results, results! So we gave him results. Lies! Just a bunch of lies!"

<Ouch,> Marco said. <Swish! Three-pointer for Cassie.>

<I so totally should have bet you guys some money,> Cassie said smugly.

"I wanted to tell him. I wanted to say, Look, it can't be done. You don't understand! There's no such thing as a human being without a free will. It's . . . it's . . . idiotic! But he's no scientist, much less a philosopher. You can't separate a sentient creature from free will. They *are* free will. Yeerk, Hork-Bajir, human, it doesn't matter. A sentient species has free will like an object has mass. You can't separate them! But Visser Three doesn't listen."

<Yes, we've noticed that,> Marco said drily. <He's really not a very nice person.>

133

<Is there another way out of here?> Prince Jake asked.

"I can't help *you*. He'll kill me," the man pleaded.

<You know, I'd probably feel sorry for you, except that guess what? You're scum! You locked these people up! These humans,> Cassie added. <We Andalites don't approve of that kind of behavior! They have families who must be tearing their —>

"No, no families that we know of. These are all street people. I'm not a fool. I knew we'd have to dispose of them in the end."

Cassie was at his throat before the human could draw his next breath. She knocked him down on his back, pressed her two front paws down on his shoulders, and bared her teeth, inches from his face.

<We do not *dispose* of humans,> Cassie said. <We need a way out of here. Right now. Or we won't leave you to Visser Three. We'll unfreeze these humans and leave you to *them*.>

"Just let me escape with you," the man pleaded. "I'd rather die of Kandrona starvation than face Visser Three."

WHAM!

WHAM!

Someone was ramming a very large, very heavy object against the outer door.

<They'll bring up some Dracon beams soon,> Marco warned. <No time!>

<We are not leaving these people behind,> Cassie said.

<No. We're not,> Prince Jake agreed. <Ax. Rachel. And me, at the door. Everyone else, bust these people loose.>

WHAM! WHAM! WHAM!

The door rattled. Bent inward.

Looking back with my stalk eyes, I saw the caged humans begin to stir. Cassie turned off the bio-stasis. The humans moved around in their cages.

"Animals! That's a bear!" one man cried.

"Yeah, well, what's *that*?" a woman said, pointing at me.

WHAM! WHAM! WHAM!

<Everyone climb out of the cages. We're getting out of here,> Prince Jake ordered.

"Says who?" a gnarled old man demanded.

<Says no one,> Cassie said gently. <Your choice. Stay or go.>

"Yeah? Well, this shelter is terrible. I'm going back to the Salvation Army," the man said.

<Hmmm,> Cassie said. <I believe that was a human being exercising free will.>

<You are going to gloat about this forever, aren't you?> Marco asked her.

<Yes. I am.>

<Okay, how do we get out of here?> Prince Jake asked the Controller scientist.

"Follow me."

We formed a bizarre parade. Cassie and me, with the scientist up front. A dozen shabby, confused, but free humans. And bringing up the rear, tensed and ready for the Yeerks to pour into the room, the rest of my friends.

<I have a question,> I told the scientist. <A scientific inquiry.>

"Andalites," he said without any particular anger. "At least your people genuinely appreciate science."

<The chimpanzees. You said your formula was ineffective because sentience cannot be separated from free will. So I must ask: Did the formula work on the chimpanzees? Are they, in fact, sentient?>

"The chimpanzees? The formula had no effect. But was it because their will remained unaffected? Or merely because there was no free will to affect? We do not know."

<I know,> Cassie said.

CHAPTER 27

"In the annals of stupid, screwed-up, pointless missions that was the stupidest, most pointless of them all," Marco said.

It was the next day. We were at the mall. In the food court.

A food court is a sort of temple of exquisite foods. I was there in human morph, naturally. Meaning that I had a mouth. Tobias was also human.

And soon, very soon, as soon as Rachel came back from standing in the lines, I would have a delicious cinnamon bun.

"I mean, all this trouble for what? For a Yeerk

plot that was already a total failure. We could have stayed home."

"We set some chimpanzees free," Cassie said. "And some humans, too, which, *Marco*, is even better."

Marco laughed. "Oh come on, you know you're a hopeless tree-hugging animal nut. Come on. You're wearing Birkenstocks right now, aren't you? Confess."

Rachel came back carrying a tray of foods. Including my delicious, incredible cinnamon bun. She handed various items to my friends.

Then, at last . . . the bun!

I began to eat it, taking care not to eat the paper plate as well, since I have learned that is considered improper.

"Here's your burger, Marco," Rachel said.

"Oh! I can't believe this. A burger?" Cassie said. "After Ax was nearly carved up? After being in that slaughterhouse?"

Marco opened his mouth wide and took a very large bite. He chewed as we all watched. The burger appeared to be juicy, with a great deal of tasty grease.

Rachel tapped her fingers on the table and stared at Marco with an indecipherable expression. Prince Jake also stared.

"Be right back," Rachel said and stood up.

"Get me one, too," Prince Jake said. "Extra pickles."

"Mmmfff!" I said, unable to make proper mouth sounds because of the large wad of unchewed cinnamon bun.

"I think that makes three," Prince Jake said.

#29 The Sickness

Marco morphed and took to the air. The rest of us watched Ax sweat and tremble.

"The Yeerks have probably figured out how we got in last time," Rachel said. "We need a new way in if we don't want to get ambushed."

"Maybe it would help if we go over everything we know about the Yeerk pool's security systems," I suggested. "We know there's the Gleet BioFilter, and —"

<Hunter-killer robots,> Tobias added.

"It was never exactly easy," Jake said. "But it's harder, now."

"There has to be a way," Rachel said.

We went over everything we knew and came up blank. And Ax still trembled.

I checked my watch. Time was running out. My parents would be home soon. First thing my dad would do was come to the barn.

<Here come Erek and Marco,> Tobias announced at last.

I glanced out the barn door. Erek and Marco, walking side by side, fast. If you saw Erek you'd think he was just a normal kid. He looks kind of like Jake, actually, only a little shorter.

But Erek's an android. Part of a race called the Chee. And what you see when you look at him, that's just a hologram. Under the hologram Erek looks a little like a robot dog walking on its hind legs.

"This is a change," Erek said. "I'm usually the one giving you guys some bad news."

"You want bad news?" Rachel said. "Ax is no better, and we can't figure out how to get into the Yeerk pool."

"Do you know anything about Andalite physiology?" I asked Erek.

He shrugged. Or at least caused his holographic self to shrug. "Nothing."

"Are any of your people surgeons?" I asked.

Erek shook his head. "The guy who plays my father? He was a doctor back in fifteenth-century France. He knows nothing useful, trust me."

"Erek, does the Yeerk pool have toilets?" Marco demanded suddenly.

"Marco, not the time," Jake muttered.

"Marco," Rachel warned, "Be useful, or be shut up."

"Come on. It's practically like a city down there," Marco continued. "They must have a place for the human hosts to take a leak or get a drink of water," he insisted.

"Sinks, toilets. They've got the works, sure," Erek answered.

The Chee are heavily programmed against violence. But that doesn't mean they don't hate the Yeerks. And they are the best spies you can imagine.

"That means they have plumbing. Pipes. And that also means we have a way into the Yeerk pool," Marco announced. "We morph into something small, something that can swim. Climb in one of our toilets, have Erek give us a flush, swim a little, and come out in one of the Yeerk sinks or toilets."

"Oh, yeah, that should work," Rachel said. "What are you, nuts?"

<The water pressure would be pretty hard to swim against,> Tobias commented.

Jake lifted his head. "Not if we started from the water tower. Then we'd go *with* the pressure all the way." He started to sound a little excited. His eyes glittered. "Erek, can you tap into the city water department computers? Combine it with . . ." Jake sighed and wiped his mouth.

"Combine it, with, um, with all you know about the Yeerk pool and . . . you know . . ."

"And give you a map? Directions?" Erek nodded. "I can give you directions to any sink or toilet in the place." He pointed at the computer my father and I use to keep records on the animals. "Mind?"

"There's no modem," I said.

Erek smiled. "Not necessary. I can be a modem."

Marco shot a triumphant glance at Rachel. "See? Still think my idea is nuts?" His face darkened. "Wait a minute. It *is* nuts. What's the matter with me? Am I insane?"

<Do we have a morph that could work?> Tobias asked.

"Maybe cockroach," I answered.

Jake shook his head. "There's a lot of pipe between the water tower and the Yeerk pool. I know they don't need to breathe much, but they do need to breathe eventually."

Tobias said, <I have an idea. Eels. They have them in tubs behind the bait shop. They're thin. And they're pretty fast, I think. Tasty.>

When I made a face, he said, <Hey, you think it's easy catching a mouse every day?>

"Eels? Do it," Jake ordered. A second later, Tobias was gone.

"Come on, Erek. We'll show you Ax's stall

where we want you to do the hologram," Marco said.

Ax was asleep. He shuffled his feet in the hay as we crowded around the low stall door, but he didn't wake up. I did a quick temperature check on him.

Ninety-five point seven. Not much of a drop. Good. He wasn't close to the crisis point yet.

"I think the best thing is for me to stay in the stall with Ax," Erek said. "I can project a hologram around us both."

He slipped into the stall and closed the door behind him. A moment later, it was like he and Ax had disappeared. The stall looked completely empty.

I leaned my head over the stall door. The air shimmered around me, then Erek and Ax appeared.

"Thanks for doing this, Erek," I said.

"No prob," he answered.

"Don't you want a book to read in there?" I asked. "It's going to be boring."

"I have several thousand books stored in my brain. Sometimes I pass the time by seeing how many I can read and comprehend at the same time."

"Ooookay. Forget I asked."

I pulled my head out of the stall. I took a closer look at the hologram protecting Ax and

Erek. No wrinkle or ripple or shadow to make my dad suspicious.

Unless he tried to go inside.

He won't, I told myself. He'd be too busy taking care of all the sick animals in cages to go poking around in an empty stall. I hoped.

"I just had a thought," Marco said.

"I'll buy you a card to commemorate the moment." Rachel, of course.

Marco didn't bother with a comeback. "If Ax goes into delirious mode, he could go running into town with underpants on his head or something. Erek won't be able to stop him."

He was right. The Chee aren't programmed for violence. Any kind of violence.

I looked at Jake. When stuff like this comes up, we all pretty much look at Jake.

Jake dropped his head back and closed his eyes for a long moment. Then he made his decision. "We've got to risk it. If something goes wrong at the Yeerk pool, it might take all of us to fight our way out."

I heard the flap of wings. Something oily slithered down my shoulder, then plopped onto the barn floor.

<Sorry,> Tobias apologized. <I dropped that thing eight times on the way back. Lost the other one completely.>

"Hence slippery as an eel," Marco joked. "By

the way, what with this being a crisis and all I'm not even going to mention the sheer, bizarre, utter stupidity of taking a long ride through the city water supply. . . . But, just for the record, this is insane!"

He picked up the eel and held it for a moment, absorbing its DNA. Then he handed it to Rachel. When she was finished, she handed it to Jake. He held it briefly, focusing, then passed it to me.

"Did you get it already?" I asked Tobias.

<Yeah,> he said. <Eels. Why don't I just keep my mouth shut? Slimy little thing. Looks like a Yeerk.>

I glanced around the group. "I feel like we're missing someone," I said.

Then it hit me. Really hit me.

Ax. We'd be doing this mission without Ax.

Visser Four ran. But he was merely a human-Controller. So there was very little chance of him outrunning me. I was still in harrier morph. I swooped through the trees as he ran.

Rising above the trees I could see the edge of a small village in the trees ahead. If Visser Four made it to the village it would be harder for me to stop him. There would be innocent humans about.

But as a harrier I could do very little to stop him.

Decision: Stay with the Visser and be helpless, or stop, demorph, and be able to attack?

The village, a collection of primitive human dwellings with roofs apparently made of grass, was very close.

First: Keep him from the village.

I flapped my wings harder and easily caught up with the running, panting, frightened Yeerk. I turned in mid-air and plunged toward him, talons down and forward.

He looked up. Dodged to the side. Not fast enough. I felt my left talon catch the side of his head.

"Aaaahhh!" he cried.

I swept past and turned to come back after him.

"Andalite filth!" he screamed. Genuinely screamed. Pure, unfiltered hatred blazing in his blue human eyes.

He hesitated. I came for him. He broke and ran. But now there were other humans surging around us. A column of men on horses was blundering through the woods seemingly heading around toward the rear of the English lines.

But there were other humans, too. They were running from the battle. Running toward the village.

I could not demorph in plain view. The Yeerk must have known this. Now he stopped and put an arrow into the simple bow he used.

He drew the arrow back and let it fly. My harrier eyes were able to see that it was poorly aimed. It blew past and I did not even need to adjust my flight.

He ran again, and I followed. Suddenly we emerged from the edge of the wood. There was an open space between the forest and the village. There appeared to be some sort of crop planted there. Villagers were calmly harvesting, going about their busy work as though nothing was happening.

Possibly they were concerned that the battle or fugitives from it might trample the crop.

These humans barely looked up from their work as soldiers, archers, and knights on horses went running past.

Certainly they did not notice Visser Four. Or me.

I swept up to Visser Four and raked his head again, laying the scalp open. He grabbed at me, but missed.

"I'll kill you!" he raged.

<Surrender now, we have you surrounded,> I bluffed. But a Yeerk does not rise to Visser rank by being a complete fool. He laughed at my silly threat.

This was a pointless battle, I knew. In this morph I could injure him but not stop him. If I stopped to morph I could well lose him.

There were two large structures in the village. One seemed to me to be essentially military. A fort of some sort. The other had a large main building with a tall tower at one end.

It was into this building that Visser Four ran. Through a tall door.

The door had been opened. He slammed it behind him. I flared my wings and pulled up, inches from smashing into the heavy-timbered door.

<Prince Jake!> I called in frustration <Tobias! Marco! Rachel! Cassie! Anyone who can hear me, please answer.>

But there was no answer. We were far from the battlefield now. I was on my own.

How to enter the large structure? How to . . .

And then, in a flash, I knew why Visser Four had returned here.

<The Time Matrix!> He'd hidden the Time Matrix in this structure! I had minutes, maybe not even that.

I landed on the stairs leading to the front door. I began to demorph. My Andalite stalk eyes began to writhe up and out of my feathered head. My fleshless bird legs grew meat and muscle and true bone. I rose, growing taller by the second. But all too slow!

Hands! I needed hands!

Tiny, limp protrusions began to grow from my chest. My forelegs. But my wings remained wings. No fingers appeared.

<Prince Jake!> I yelled again.

Visser Four was going to escape.

<Prince Jake! Rachel! Cassie!>

Now, at last, fingers! But too weak, too delicate and unformed to turn the heavy iron handle on the door.

"Aiiiieeee!" someone screamed.

A human. Perhaps upset at the sight of an Andalite struggling to emerge from . . .

"Tuez le! Tuez le!" a new voice screamed.

"Tuez le!" Now it was a chorus. I twisted one stalk eye, only now beginning to work.

There were half a dozen humans. Some were soldiers. Others not. The ones who were soldiers brandished swords. The others held huge forks made of sharpened wood.

I was quite sure they were not welcoming me to their town.

<Prince Jake!> I cried. I lurched on half-formed legs to reach the door. My weak fingers closed on the handle. The angry villagers attacked.

ANIMORPHS

Someone has found the Time Matrix. Unfortunately, he is a human-Controller named Henry. Even worse, until a recent demotion, Henry was known as Visser Four.

With the Time Matrix, Henry has his big chance to regain power: He'll alter history and win Earth for the Yeerks. Not knowing too much about human history, Henry lands in the middle of what humans refer to as "World War II." With the Ellimist's help, the Animorphs must travel back in time to stop Henry before it's too late. But in the process, one Animorph must die...

<MEGAMORPHS #3>: Elfangor's Secret

K.A. Applegate

Starring all six characters!

Visit the Web site at
http://www.scholastic.com/animorphs

SCHOLASTIC

The Ax is about to fall...

ANIMORPHS

K. A. Applegate

There's something wrong with Ax. Seriously wrong. He's got a virus and it's killing him. It's up to Cassie and the other Animorphs to find a cure—and save his life—without giving their secret away.

ANIMORPHS #29: THE SICKNESS

Watch Animorphs on Television!